The Undoing *of* My Marriage

A Woman's Search for Fulfilment in the Grey Space Between Commitment and Freedom – Based on True Events

AJ Moore

Copyright © 2025 A J Moore

The moral right of the author has been asserted.

Apart from any fair dealing for the purposes of research or private study, or criticism or review, as permitted under the Copyright, Designs and Patents Act 1988, this publication may only be reproduced, stored or transmitted, in any form or by any means, with the prior permission in writing of the publishers, or in the case of reprographic reproduction in accordance with the terms of licences issued by the Copyright Licensing Agency. Enquiries concerning reproduction outside those terms should be sent to the publishers.

The manufacturer's authorised representative in the EU
for product safety is Authorised Rep Compliance Ltd,
71 Lower Baggot Street, Dublin D02 P593 Ireland (www.arccompliance.com)

This is a work of fiction. Names, characters, businesses, places, events and incidents are either the products of the author's imagination or used in a fictitious manner. Any resemblance to actual persons, living or dead, or actual events is purely coincidental.

Troubador Publishing Ltd
Unit E2 Airfield Business Park,
Harrison Road, Market Harborough,
Leicestershire. LE16 7UL
Tel: 0116 2792299
Email: books@troubador.co.uk
Web: www.troubador.co.uk

ISBN 978-1-83628-470-3

British Library Cataloguing in Publication Data.
A catalogue record for this book is available from the British Library.

Printed and bound in Great Britain by 4edge Limited
Typeset in 11pt Adobe Garamond Pro by Troubador Publishing Ltd, Leicester, UK

To my daughter: I said you weren't allowed to read the book Mum wrote about 'grown-up things'! If you do, I hope you're much, much older, and have found your own version of fulfilment. Thank you for being my anchor, even when I'm somewhere in the unknown.

To my friend Marcus: One of the few who knew the full, uncensored version of my story before this book. Thank you for always listening, and for lending a male perspective.

And finally, to my test reader: I think we've been a test for each other in a number of ways! I'm grateful our paths crossed. P.S. I hope you don't skip the poems this time.

PROLOGUE

Caterpillars in the Dark

My skin crawls as my husband's fingertips trace circles on my right hip. My pelvic floor tenses, as if bracing itself against him. I know what those circles mean.

"Not tonight. It's too late," I say, removing his hand. "You took an hour to come to bed tonight," I chastise him.

I'd even told him earlier that we should plan to have sex tonight. It's not my fault he always spends so long on his computer and then takes forever in the bathroom before finally joining me. What does he even do in there? My body feels heavy and numb after half falling asleep waiting for him. I switch off the bedside lamp. The mattress creaks as he shifts further over to his side of the bed.

I sigh. It's been three weeks since we last had sex. If we don't tonight, it will be the same story tomorrow night, and the night after that. More weeks will pass, and before we know it, we'll be one of *those* couples – the sexless marriage ones I swore we'd never become.

Reluctantly, I slide closer to my husband. Reaching my hand around his waist, I slip my hand under the elastic waistband of his briefs and grasp his soft cock. I stroke it, half-heartedly, for what feels like several minutes, feeling myself grow impatient as it remains flaccid.

He turns to face me and fumbles around to locate my breasts in the darkness. It used to turn me on when he'd fondle them and gently squeeze my nipples, but now the sensation feels almost irritating, leaving my pussy stubbornly dry.

I glance at the alarm clock on my bedside table: 11.44pm. If we finish by midnight, I might get six hours of sleep before I have to get up for work. Anything less, and I won't be able to function. I nudge my husband onto his back and kiss him. His breath has a stale taste, and his tongue feels slimy in my mouth.

"Have you noticed kissing feels weird now?" I blurt out, pulling my lips away. I'm aware I'm killing the barely there mood.

"In what way?" he asks.

I don't know how to explain it. Our lips reconnect clumsily, like out-of-sync dancers. Our mouths are a mixing bowl of saliva. When did kissing him get so sloppy? I pull off our underwear and straddle him in the cowgirl position. He's finally hard enough – just. Adjusting his semi-on inside me, I grind back and forth. At least I come quickly this way. My orgasm is sharp and sweet; a contrast to my numbness, but a lot of effort for little reward, it seems.

I climb off my husband and lie prone, my face buried

in the pillow. He fucks me from behind, his breath heaving against my back as he finishes. I let out an obligatory moan.

Wedging a tissue between my thighs, I scurry to the bathroom down the hallway and close the door. *At least that's out of the way for a while*, I think, wiping off his semen.

> *His fingertips used to set a hundred butterflies on flight.*
> *Now they feel like caterpillars crawling over my skin,*
> *making me shudder as I wonder*
> *how butterflies could turn into caterpillars.*

CHAPTER 1

Take Me Back

I remember the first time I ever saw you.
How were you once a stranger?
I remember the look in your eyes when you first saw me.
How magical it was, when we couldn't tear our eyes away.
I remember the first time you kissed me,
how I explored your body with my hands,
and you explored mine;
how thrilling it was to discover each other.
I remember the first time we exchanged 'I love you'.
How those words had such weight back then.
Three words repeated so often now;
how they've lost their meaning over the years.
I remember the first time I realised you would be my last;
how perfect it felt, my heart never so certain.
All those memories of us, I'll never forget.
How I long though, to have those first times again.

Like many early relationships, we couldn't get enough of each other during those first few months. When we were together, it felt like we were the only two people in the world. We'd often spend entire days in the bedroom with the curtains drawn – lust-filled hours of sex and lying together in naked bliss.

When we were apart, he was always on my mind. I physically ached for him, living for the next time I'd see him. We'd text constantly, telling each other how much we couldn't wait to be together again. I thought I'd been in love before, but nothing had ever felt as intense or *reciprocated* as it did with him.

"You'll just know when it's the right person," my mother had told me when I was single and worried that I'd never find 'the one'. She was right. I did 'just know'.

Until I didn't.

I'd been so excited to find the love of my life at twenty-five – especially after my previous boyfriend had left me heartbroken – that I rushed the relationship forward at whirlwind speed.

Four months after meeting, I moved into the flat he shared with a few of his friends.

And not long after, we (namely me) decided it would be nicer just the two of us, so we found a rental on our own.

I'd never lived alone with a partner before and, at the time, it felt like the most exciting step we could take. At first, it was everything I imagined. I'd cook him elaborate meals without the hassle of sharing a kitchen with flatmates. We no longer had to be mindful of the headboard banging against the wall. We could fuck on the couch in the middle of the day.

It was total freedom – this little domestic universe of ours. It didn't take long for little tensions to creep in though.

"Dinner's ready," I remember calling out one night. He was gaming on his computer in our bedroom, as he usually did after work.

"Be there in a minute," he replied. "Just about to kill this last boss."

I'd never really *gotten* gaming, but it seemed to be his favourite pastime. "He'll stop once you have kids – they grow out of it," my friends with husbands and families had assured me. Spoiler alert: he didn't.

Despite my reminders, at least half an hour passed before he finally came out to the living room.

"Your dinner will be cold by now," I said, casting my eyes down at my empty plate on my lap.

"I'm sorry, AJ, it took longer than I thought," he said, sitting down beside me on the couch. "Thanks for dinner."

Even though it bothered me, I brushed it aside at the time, unaware of how his video game obsession would grate on me in the years to come.

Renting was another point of contention. As we acquired more things together, our unit was starting to feel cramped and overcrowded.

"Let's find something bigger and more modern," I'd suggested one night. "It will be worth paying more rent for."

"We need to buy our own house, instead of paying someone else's mortgage," he said, ignoring the rental listing I was trying to show him on my phone.

I told him I'd rather be married first before we bought a house together; it seemed more traditional. We'd discussed the idea of getting married in vague terms before then. Not so much the technicalities, but we were unanimous in that we wanted to spend the rest of our lives together.

The following weekend we were doing some shopping at the mall when he steered me towards a jewellery store.

"Pick your engagement ring," he told me, with a bashful grin.

A week later, six months after meeting, we went out for dinner at a noisy Japanese restaurant.

"Will you marry me?" he'd asked, as he self-consciously pulled out the box with the ring I'd chosen. His voice was barely audible over the echo of rowdy tables.

"Yes!" I replied. I couldn't wait to update my Facebook status to *Engaged* and share the news with everyone.

I carried a tinge of disappointment about that night over the years though. It would've been nice to have that romantic, surprise proposal with the man on one knee professing his love to me. *Life isn't the movies though*, I reminded myself.

***

For the entire year before it, I obsessed over choosing the perfect dress, colour scheme, and music. My eyes would fill with tears as I imagined how beautiful I'd look standing at the altar, reciting the heartfelt poems I'd written before we exchanged vows.

In my head, the perfect wedding was symbolic of our love – I wanted to show everyone there how right we were for each other. Every detail felt like a reflection of us. Those poems weren't just words, they were a testament to how deep and committed our love was. And, admittedly, a way for our wedding to stand out from the rest in its authenticity. "AJ wrote those herself?" I pictured our guests whispering to one another, marvelling at how original and moving our wedding was.

Apart from managing only three hours of sleep the night before – thanks to all my nervous excitement – our wedding day went perfectly. Everything came together just as I'd hoped, maybe even better.

"It's been even better than I expected!" I said to my husband in a quiet moment we'd stolen away from the crowd.

That night, we were both exhilarated and exhausted after hours of photos, talking to guests, eating, drinking, and dancing. By the time the wedding ended at around midnight, we collapsed on the bed in our hotel suite.

"Do you think it matters if we don't have sex on our wedding night?" I asked him.

"No, of course not," my husband said without hesitation. "It's been a huge day. I'm shattered."

I remember giving my new husband a quick peck on the lips before we fell asleep, my wedding-night lingerie still packed in my suitcase.

Maybe we should've done it anyway – it seems wrong that we didn't, I'd thought the next morning, a faint unease settling over me as I woke. Strangely, this was the first time I recall thinking about sex as something I was obliged to do, even if I didn't feel like it.

Take me back to that night in the bar,
the first time I ever saw you.
The moment you stopped being a stranger,
the thrill of meeting someone new.

Take me back to our drunken courtship,
our dancing bodies entwined.
Intoxicated by lust,
fireworks blazing in my mind.

Take me back to when I still missed you,
when we'd text each other till late at night.
When your goodnight 'X's on my phone
would set my heart alight.

Take me back to when we said 'I love you',
and I felt the weight of those words to my core.
So convinced our love would last forever.
Just take me back to before I wasn't sure.

CHAPTER 2

The Truth About Marriage

The post-wedding blues hit me faster than my rose bouquet wilted and died. I'd spent so much time and energy on planning the wedding that once it was over, I had no idea how to occupy my mind.

I also struggled to reconcile that I'd finally attained the thing society had told me I needed to chase: somebody who *chose* me. If my love life was one of my husband's video games, then achieving the feat of getting married felt like conquering the final 'boss'. *What's the end goal now?* I'd wondered.

The only way I can describe how I felt then is *empty*. It's not technically an emotion, but it perfectly described my state – devoid of anything to plan or fixate on. It felt familiar, like my default setting, one I'd fallen back on since I was very young.

"You're depressed," my mother would tell me whenever she'd notice me looking glum, or lost in my own thoughts, which were far too introspective, even as a child.

I always found it dismissive – how she reduced the complexity of my feelings to an overused diagnosis that didn't quite fit. To me, it felt like a giant hole inside me, perpetually searching for something to fill it, rather than simply a persistent sadness.

"I'm not depressed," I repeated to her over the years. "I'm not sad all the time. And I always want to get up in the morning."

Back then, I held on to that reasoning, refusing to take medication or 'see someone' for a condition I believed I didn't have. My understanding of depression was limited then, though. It would take years before I realised it could manifest as so much more than sadness.

A few months after our wedding, my husband and I went to Fiji for our honeymoon. It was nice, even though the bad weather dampened things a bit. Still, walking around as a married couple felt different. Something about our energy together had shifted – it didn't feel as *sexy* anymore. We were no longer the young, starry-eyed lovers we'd been on our wedding day. Instead, we were just another married couple on holiday. For something sold as the ultimate fairy-tale ending, it felt disappointingly ordinary.

When we returned, we started house-hunting and applied for a mortgage, which turned out to be incredibly stressful and caused plenty of arguments. After months of missing out on properties, we finally had an offer accepted and moved into our first home. It was a three-bedroom 1960s house that reeked of smoke when we moved in. The carpet was filthy, the wallpaper was peeling off, and behind it were patches of disgusting black mould.

"Won't take much to tidy it up," my dad said confidently, forgetting that we had zero experience in DIY compared to his years of flipping houses.

Even though our house was far from perfect, it was ours. I wondered if, had we bought it a couple of years earlier, we would have wanted to 'christen' every room. Now, I had no such desire. Married sex, it turned out, wasn't as hot – at least not for us.

We still had sex several times a week back then, but it had definitely lost some of its fire. I found myself wishing he'd be more spontaneous – just come home from work, grab me, and throw me down on the bed. But that wasn't him. Most of the time, if we had sex at any time other than bedtime, it was because I initiated it.

Maybe it was just the effects of long-term cohabitation, but my feelings for him started to shift. What once felt romantic now felt overly familiar – too platonic. It was hard to pinpoint exactly when it started, but the change was disconcerting. I still loved him, though.

Admittedly, I didn't feel like he was my 'soulmate', but he was my best friend. Yet I couldn't shake the feeling that something was missing. It occurred to me that the timing of our wedding had coincided with the two-year mark of our relationship – right when the 'honeymoon phase' supposedly ends. I couldn't help but wonder, *would I have been so certain about marrying him if we'd taken things more slowly back then?*

"All relationships go like that eventually, AJ," my mother said when I confided in her that married life wasn't what I'd expected.

"Remember when I told you things would change, that you'd end up like your dad and me someday?"

She wasn't wrong – I had criticised her and my father for staying married despite bickering constantly and rarely showing each other affection.

"You're wrong," I'd insisted at the time. "We'll never end up like you and Dad."

"Your dad and I were like you two once," she retorted. "Marriage takes a lot of work."

> *"But how will I know," you asked, "that he's the right one?"*
> *"You'll just know," they said. "It will just feel right."*
> *And one day you finally meet him,*
> *and the 'rightness' hits you like a lightning bolt.*
> *Then the honeymoon phase passes –*
> *you swore it never would, not for you –*
> *but the sparks die and the doubts arise.*
> *You start to see cracks appear,*
> *where once there was perfection.*
> *You're discontent, dissatisfied, disappointed.*
> *It doesn't matter what you call it though –*
> *they're all just synonyms,*
> *for falling out of love.*
> *"But what went wrong?" you ask.*
> *"Marriage takes a lot of work," they say.*
> *"Why didn't you tell me?" you ask.*
> *Then you remember; they did.*
> *You didn't listen though –*
> *you thought yours was the exception.*

CHAPTER 3

Paradox

*You've seen all the light inside me.
Yet when you still loved me
after I showed you the shadows;
that's how I knew,
you're a keeper.*

A baby seemed like the next logical step for us. The timing of her wasn't exactly planned, but she wasn't an accident either. 'Surprise baby' felt like the most fitting term.

I'd never been sure if I wanted children. With my tendency toward anxiety and feeling easily overwhelmed by life's pressures, parenting always seemed like *a lot*. Yet, in my late twenties, I started experiencing maternal urges I'd never felt before. I admired my pregnant coworkers – it was true, pregnant women really did glow. There was something radiant yet grounded about them, an earthy feminine energy that I found myself longing to embody.

I daydreamed about having my own cute little bump and even started making lists of baby names.

"We need to save more money first," my husband said when I'd suggested we start trying.

Another year passed, and with more money in the bank to cover baby expenses and my maternity leave, we decided to try. After two unsuccessful cycles, though, I got cold feet.

"I don't think I'm ready anyway," I'd said, tossing my second negative pregnancy test in the bin. "Maybe we can wait another year. We need to finish doing up the house and should travel some more first, anyway."

I couldn't explain the abrupt change of heart. But suddenly, all the unknowns of having a baby seemed like something I wasn't sure I could handle. *What if I hated my body afterwards? What if there were complications? What if I just couldn't manage the responsibility of caring for a child?* I just couldn't seem to get these worries out of my mind.

I didn't go back on the pill, though. Instead, we used condoms for protection on the days my menstrual tracking app said I was fertile. This method gave us a false sense of security for six months, until my period didn't arrive on its due date like it normally would.

I'd called in sick to work that morning because I'd slept terribly and felt a bit off. Naturally, I decided to take a pregnancy test. When it showed two blue lines, I could hardly believe it. I called my husband at work straight away.

"I'm pregnant!" I exclaimed as soon as he answered. There was silence for a few moments.

"Oh fuck, AJ, we're having a baby!" he finally responded, his voice matching the mix of shock and excitement I felt inside.

Despite still not feeling quite ready, as soon as I found out I was expecting, I couldn't wait to be a mum. But all the hormonal changes took their toll, exacerbating my mood swings like crazy. For the first trimester, I was angry, irritable, tearful, and irrational. And my husband bore the brunt of it. I berated him for spending too much time gaming on weekends instead of working on the house renovations.

"The baby's room and the lounge aren't even nearly finished!" I'd accused him. "We can't focus on a baby if the house is a complete mess!"

"I work all week; I need some time to fucking relax!" he snapped back. "Maybe you could help more too!"

So, I helped him strip wallpaper and paint the walls, but my nausea and fatigue made me feel a bit useless. I wished I could just chill and enjoy my pregnancy, but I wanted everything to be perfect for when our baby arrived.

Along with the nausea, I developed food aversions to almost everything I'd enjoyed eating before. I'd always been health-conscious and wanted to eat all the right nutrients while pregnant, but it became nearly impossible when I could no longer stomach meat, salad, cooked vegetables, or even cereal.

"You haven't brushed your teeth properly," I'd complained to my husband, turning my face away when he tried to kiss me in bed.

"I've brushed my teeth twice, and I've used mouthwash," he'd sigh. But it made no difference – I had developed an aversion to my own husband too. I never saw that listed as a pregnancy symptom.

Minus the kissing, we tried to maintain a regular sex life until I was about seven months along, when my bump really started to show. Then, he said he felt 'weird' being so close to the baby's head, so we didn't have sex again while I was pregnant.

The day our daughter was born, all the frustration and resentment from the past nine months melted away. It felt like we were united again in our shared love and excitement for her.

"You were amazing," my husband said, squeezing my hand adoringly after witnessing me in labour and giving birth. I felt amazing too – like I'd just acquired superpowers or climbed Mount Everest. Our daughter was beautiful and perfect, and I fell in love with her the moment my midwife placed her tiny, vernix-covered body in my arms.

On the drive home from the hospital two days later, I glanced back at our daughter in her capsule. It hit me then, the reality that we were now a family of three, heading home to an uncharted life together. And there was no turning back.

> *I used to hold onto you so tight*
> *that we started to feel like one,*
> *then I started to detach,*
> *like a shadow cast in the sun.*
> *Now part of me tries to break away,*
> *but the other part sticks like glue,*
> *unsure of who I would be*
> *if I wasn't attached to you.*

After having my baby suckling on my breasts for hours each day, the last thing I wanted was my husband's hands or mouth anywhere near them. I loved my daughter, but after seven months of being at home on maternity leave, I felt like I'd lost myself to motherhood and was completely touched out.

"I might switch her to formula so you can have a turn feeding her sometimes," I told my husband after the third time she'd woken up one night. She always wanted night feeds, but I'd never had much success pumping milk, so giving her a bottle of formula seemed like a good alternative.

"But we agreed you'd breastfeed her exclusively for a year!" he protested.

It was true; before she was born, we had both been determined to only give her breastmilk until she turned one, in line with the take-home 'breast is best' message from antenatal classes. But I'd had no idea how physically and mental demanding breastfeeding would be.

"It's my body!" I cried, my agitation heightened by chronic sleep deprivation. "I literally get no break from her!"

We argued back and forth about him being too stubborn and inflexible, and me always going back on my word – a recurring theme in our relationship.

The baby stage didn't last forever, thankfully. I eventually got unbroken sleep again, along with my slim, fit, pre-pregnancy body. When I enrolled our daughter in daycare and returned to work, I realised I was much more suited to being a working mum than a stay-at-home one.

Up with the birds this morning,
gazing out the window at the sleepy sky,
sipping coffee, savouring the solitude,
before the moment she'll start to cry.
Up with the birds this morning,

watching them fly and be free,
while I'm caged in by motherhood.
I wanted her, I know,
but sometimes I miss being me.

***

I'd just entered my early thirties at the time, and I was more confident and self-assured than ever; more attractive, too. Or maybe it was just that the insecurities of my teens and twenties had faded, and I'd finally found my own sense of style.

I felt more elegant, more refined, and with the early stages of motherhood behind me, I started to feel sexual again. It was different though, as if a powerful, sensual energy had suddenly emerged inside me.

When she walks now,
her hips sway to the rhythm
of a tune only she can hear.
Her lips are dressed in red
and she wears a satisfied smile,
as if hiding a special secret.
Fire burns in her veins,
and her eyes gleam like glitter,
reflecting her glow within.
She can't help but do a little dance
when she passes by a mirror –
this is how it feels, she thinks,
to be alive.

But this new force didn't fit with the monotony of my role as the mother of a young child, nor did it translate to my mundane marriage to a man I had lost all sexual attraction for. It became restless, a growing energy I couldn't ignore. It needed an outlet.

At first, that outlet came in the form of harmless daydreams about men I'd notice around work – simple moments of attraction, a quick glance exchanged. When my husband and I had sex, I found myself closing my eyes and imagining what it would be like to be with someone else. *How good it would feel*, I'd think, *to fuck someone I really wanted again.*

> *You're like that red dress hanging in my closet.*
> *I bet you'd look amazing on;*
> *but who am I to think I could wear something so daringly sexy?*
> *I've been seeing you in passing for a while now.*
> *I try to retain my composure as I feel the heat rising in my cheeks,*
> *and drive myself crazy over-analysing the tone you say hi to me in.*
> *Our conversations have never extended beyond an exchange of greetings.*
> *Maybe it's better that way though.*
> *You're much older than I am, but maybe that's the attraction.*
> *There's something about a man in a suit who looks like he's lived a little.*
> *Tall, dark and handsome, you're all the clichés of a*

Hollywood heart-throb.
Real life isn't like the movies though – there are always boundaries, rules to follow.
If only I could stop my knees going weak when you say my name.
And not melt when you smile at me or return your inviting gaze.
All I can do is remind myself of the diamond ring on my finger.
It wouldn't go with that red dress at all.

I did my best to repress my desires, my growing discontentment. I couldn't understand how the fire that had once burnt so strong for my husband had been completely extinguished.

"It's normal," I told myself, going through the motions of keeping up appearances as a happily married couple.

But I couldn't trick my body. It increasingly rejected my husband. When he leaned down to kiss my mouth, I'd turn away so his lips would land on my cheek instead. If he walked in on me getting dressed, I'd cover my breasts – I just didn't want to be naked in front of him. We still had sex, but it felt like a task, something to get done rather than something I wanted.

It wasn't my libido. I often felt intensely horny, in fact, just not for my husband. I started 'taking care of it' when I came home from work during my lunch break, one of the only times I had the house to myself. I felt guilty, though, getting more pleasure alone than I did with him. And despite the multiple orgasms I gave myself, I still felt unsatisfied.

I tried to visualise the years ahead, when our daughter would've left home, and it would be just the two of us again. If we already felt like a passionless, stale couple in our thirties, I dreaded how much worse it would surely get by the time we reached our sixties.

But we were married, we had a child – our entire lives were bound together. I couldn't just leave it all behind for some unknown alternative life, just for the chance to feel desire for someone again.

"Everything is fine," I repeated to myself, never quite convinced.

Within this bond we share
lies the ultimate paradox:
a life created,
histories merged,
a commitment made
to do this for life.
A love so safe and familiar,
it's my forever home.
Yet my heart wants to explore,
to adventure,
to discover more –
forever unsatisfied.

CHAPTER 4

Pills

In addition to my anxiety over the state of my marriage, I found myself struggling with the decision of whether or not to have another child. After the first few years of our daughter's life, I felt relieved to be out of the trenches – no more nappies, potty training, nap schedules, or the all-encompassing responsibility of having a small human entirely dependent on me.

My husband was undeniably a great dad, but I couldn't help envying friends when they raved how their husbands would take over parenting duties as soon as they got home from work, or give them a break by taking the kids out for a few hours on the weekend.

My husband left for work in the mornings before our daughter woke up, leaving me to juggle getting her fed and dressed for daycare while also trying to get myself ready for work. It wasn't easy, and there were plenty of mornings filled with tears and meltdowns – both hers and mine.

On the tougher days, I'd sigh with relief when I got back

to my car after dropping her off. As awful as it felt to admit, my workday felt like a blissful escape, only having to worry about myself for a while.

My husband would come home at night after I'd already finished work, picked up our daughter from daycare, and started our evening routine. We then took turns exercising in the garage while the other played with her inside. I usually went first, so by the time he was doing his workout, I had to juggle keeping our daughter entertained with getting dinner on the table. Since my husband never liked cooking, that task always fell to me, while he did the dishes. This arrangement also meant I was the one doing our daughter's bedtime routine most nights while he was busy cleaning up.

He'd give her a quick hug and kiss goodnight, but I couldn't help feeling like he got off lightly compared to the demands I faced as a working mother. I'd always believed parenting should be an equal partnership but achieving that seemed impossible.

***

With each year that passed, I wrestled with the guilt of not giving our daughter a sibling. Every month, as if on cue, maternal urges surged with my ovulation, clashing head on with my conviction that we were fine as a family of three – that one child was all I could handle. Mid-month, I'd insist we try for another baby.

"She needs a sibling," I'd argue. "It's selfish to just have one."

"You just said last week you couldn't handle another," my husband would reply, sighing as though he'd heard it all before.

He was right, of course – I'd had the same revelation every month since our daughter was a year old. But in those moments, it felt like a completely different person had spoken those words. I couldn't recall ever feeling that way. *Of course I could manage another baby. It would be easier the second time around*, I'd convince myself.

He'd always told me it was essentially my decision, being the mother, so he'd go along with whatever I wanted in the end. I think, deep down, he did want another child. He'd get a little excited when I speculated about whether we'd have a boy or a girl, or when I suggested baby names. But after a night of unprotected sex, I'd wake up in a panic, praying it hadn't worked.

"You need to make a decision and stick with it," he'd tell me, his voice sharp with frustration.

He wasn't inside my head, living with the constant back and forth. I think I just wished he'd make the decision for me.

"You should go see someone about your anxiety," he'd suggest, as he had so many times over the last few years. I'd consider it. I'd even book an appointment with a therapist. But a couple of weeks later, predictably, I'd cancel it the day before.

"I feel much better now," I'd tell him. "I don't even know what I'd talk to them about."

"Whatever you say," he'd reply, his indifference becoming almost a coping mechanism.

When our daughter turned four, the periods when I felt depressed and anxious began to far outweigh the moments I felt 'much better'. Aside from the second-child dilemma, I felt like I could never fully relax anywhere because of the intrusive thoughts of freak accidents or unspeakable things harming our daughter – or killing me, leaving her motherless. I finally went to my GP, who prescribed me Sertraline.

After a few weeks of feeling even more depressed and on-edge, in addition to exhausted, sick, and spaced out, I started to feel normal again. Not just normal, better than normal. I felt calmer, more rational, as though nothing could faze me anymore. To my relief, the spiralling thought loops about having another child nearly vanished.

After all, I'd rationalised; our daughter was thriving as an only child. We could afford to live comfortably, even take her on overseas holidays – why rock the boat? So, I decided to have an IUD inserted. In turn, it suppressed the ovulation hormones that had sparked my broodiness each month. It occurred to me then that maybe I genuinely had wanted another baby – just not with him. It seemed like a logical conclusion to draw.

I'd hoped the Sertraline might improve my feelings toward my husband, but, unfortunately, it didn't.On the contrary, I didn't seem to have any emotions about him at all – or anything, really. After years of being ruled by emotional turbulence, living in this blunted state wasn't the worst thing. I told my husband that my sustained lack of sexual desire was probably just a side effect of the medication. Sometimes, it's easier to live in denial.

Swallowed the last one in the packet today.
Whether they've made a difference is hard to say.
I suppose I feel… okay compared to before.
Surely it won't hurt to get some more?
Except… I can't remember the last time I cried,
not even about sad things, like when somebody died.
Been a while since I cared enough to start a fight –
guess that means they're working though, right?
In the GP's office, he brings up a questionnaire –
wait, don't they normally just dish them out here?
He asks if I've felt panicky, worried, a sense of doom?
I don't know, but the correct answer is 'often', I assume.
He calculates my score – good, I've passed the test.
"You still have anxiety," he says. "Another course will be best."
He hands me my prescription. I thank him and go.
Should be pleased… don't feel anything though.

CHAPTER 5

Seeing Grey

Now I'm always on the go,
planning our next holiday.
You tell me I should relax, take it slow,
but won't life get boring that way?
Now I'm always fighting off itchy feet –
will they ever settle down?
How are you so content and upbeat,
while I dream of moving to a different town?
Now I'm always wistful about me and you,
how fun staying put with you used to be.
It didn't matter where we'd go or what we'd do –
just being together was enough for me.

From then on, instead of planning for babies, I planned holidays. There was something about organising an overseas trip that inspired me, giving me respite from the tedium of everyday life. I'd always enjoyed going somewhere new, escaping reality for a week or so to experience a different place and culture. But my life had started to feel so claustrophobic that having travel plans to look forward to became a necessity.

While my husband gamed in the study each night after our daughter went to bed, I'd sit in the lounge on my laptop, obsessively researching destinations, tourist attractions, creating budgets, and mapping out itineraries. I'd visited Paris during my UK working holiday in my early twenties, but the rest of France seemed amazing, with its beautiful countryside and castles. I excitedly shared my idea with my husband. He had never shared my passion for travel but agreed on the premise that we'd save up all the money first, instead of putting it on credit. Within a few weeks, I'd gone off the idea and had my heart set on another destination.

"I've decided we'll do an Australian trip instead," I informed him. "It'll be cheaper, so we can go sooner," I explained. "Plus, I just think it'll be better to leave somewhere as far away as France until she's older."

My husband, however, was not enthused by the sudden change of plans.

"That's not fair," he complained. "You can't get me set on one place, and then completely switch to somewhere else."

"But it was my idea in the first place! It's not like anything was set in stone," I protested.

"But you always do this!" he accused me. "You're constantly changing your mind from one week to the next!"

"At least I come up with ideas for us! When was the last time you suggested anything?"

"For fuck's sake, AJ," he muttered under his breath before storming out of the room.

It didn't take long for these kinds of discussions to escalate. As it happened though, not long afterward, the Covid-19 pandemic hit, New Zealand's borders were closed, and we couldn't go anywhere.

During the weeks-long lockdown New Zealand was thrown into, our days were consumed with keeping our daughter entertained, taking walks around the neighbourhood, and indulging in copious amounts of baking and arts and crafts. I was grateful that we weren't financially impacted, like so many others, but I struggled with the disconnection from friends, work colleagues, our parents and siblings, as well as the uncertainty of not knowing when it would all end.

> *Someday I'll live,*
> *like a caged bird released.*
> *I'll sing my freedom from the rooftops,*
> *and navigate the edge of cliffs,*
> *with no fear of falling.*
> *I'll spread my wings wide*
> *and feel my heart bursting in my chest,*
> *as I soar above the clouds.*
> *But for now, I'll keep on walking*
> *amongst familiar places.*
> *Wings clipped; feet firmly planted*
> *upon low-lying ground.*
> *And I'll quash my soul's yearnings,*
> *as I repeat to myself over and over:*
> *this is enough.*

Being confined mostly to life within the walls of our house forced me to confront the shifted dynamics between myself and my husband even more. *There's nothing there anymore*, a voice in my mind would taunt me, *if you loved him, you wouldn't feel so trapped being stuck in the house with him*. Thoughts like these played over and over, with growing resolve. There was nothing I could do to change anything, though.

"If this goes on for another week, I'm going to lose my fucking mind," I told my husband, right before a further extension to the lockdown was announced.

> *Just inhale, count to five,*
> *exhale, start again.*
> *You've been breathing all your life,*
> *yet somehow doing it wrong.*
> *Don't always imagine the worst.*
> *(But hasn't the worst happened before?)*
> *Stop thinking in black and white,*
> *it's not all good, nor all bad, you know.*
> *Don't be ruled by your emotions,*
> *that hasn't gotten you anywhere.*
> *Stop dwelling on the past,*
> *you can't change it, after all.*
> *Try not to focus on the future,*
> *as if you can control it.*
> *So here I am, sitting in my present,*
> *being mindful, breathing slow,*
> *feeling nothing, seeing grey.*

CHAPTER 6

Greener Grass

It starts as a breeze that whispers among the trees,
about a curious ripple in the ocean.

Leaves tremble in anticipation,
while the clouds multiply and dance in the sky.

The whisper turns up, as loud as thunder:
"Brace yourself," it says.
"A storm is coming."

How was I to know, though,
that the ripples you made would become waves,
and crash upon my life like a tsunami?

His name is David, and he's 'liked' two of my new Instagram posts and started following me. He's also sent me a message.

I had only created my new Instagram account a few days ago, prompted by a trip to Queenstown over a weekend in early August with a girlfriend. It was the first time I'd left my daughter for more than one night, and the first time I'd travelled anywhere on a plane since we had finally come out of lockdown a few months ago. With the international borders still closed, I had wanted to make the most of being allowed to travel domestically again, at least. My Facebook, however, had become full of family photos, and I wanted my Instagram to be just for me.

The photos David had liked were of me standing on a bridge, smiling, in a black puffer jacket and skinny jeans, with snow-laden mountains in the background, and a selfie of me in a bikini, holding a glass of wine in a hot tub. I guess he'd come across them through the Queenstown hashtags I'd added. Curiosity stirring inside me, I open his message in my inbox.

Hey, AJ, nice photos! I was in New Zealand on vacation last year. I loved Queenstown – it's beautiful there!

According to David's bio, he lives in Boston in the United States. Scrolling down his page, there are mostly photos of various places in Boston and New York, as well as travel photos from parts of Europe and Asia. He seems to enjoy hiking.

I study one of the photos showing his face. He appears to be around my age, with short, mousey-brown hair, white skin, a medium build – on the shorter side, even – objectively average-looking, but I like that he has a boyish quality about him and kind hazel eyes. He seems worldly, politically engaged, and his captions are intelligent, thoughtful commentaries on the places he's been.

I follow him back and return to my inbox.

Hi, David, thanks for the message! I reply. *Yeah, that was just on a trip with my friend last week; it was amazing down there! How long were you here for? It's sad the borders are closed now and no tourists can visit.*

I'm surprised to see, only a few minutes later, that David is online and typing a response.

I was there for a couple of weeks, he says, *I'd love to visit again one day! Tell me about you, AJ. Where do you live?*

I decide it wouldn't be very sensible to reveal my exact location to him.

I live in the North Island, not that far from Auckland, with my husband and daughter.

Congratulations on the marriage and daughter, AJ! David says. *You're so lucky.*

He goes on to tell me that he was previously married but has been divorced for seven years. He's single, works in IT, and doesn't have any children.

I tease him about how I can trust he isn't a Nigerian scammer or something, to which he responds with a crying-with-laughter emoji.

I could ask you the same, AJ; maybe it's you who is actually the Nigerian scammer, posting fake photos of a very beautiful woman. He adds a wink at the end.

David's compliment makes me blush. It's been a long time since a man who isn't my husband has called me 'beautiful', and I have to admit, it's nice… and exciting. I can't help but smile to myself as we continue the banter.

David asks what I'm interested in.

I used to love to travel before Covid… I'm also into fitness and hiking. I've recently taken up writing poetry as well!

Very creative! What kind of poems?

Mostly about motherhood, love, marriage… just life, I guess.

That's amazing, AJ, I'd love to read them sometime!

I tell David I'm going to start a second Instagram account to share my poems soon.

It'll be anonymous. I don't want anyone I know in real life to see it.

I hope you'll let me see it. Are you happy, AJ?

His question takes me by surprise. It takes me a few moments to come up with a response.

I'm not sure. I mean, I should be happy. I have a good husband, I guess, a nice life… I don't know, sometimes I feel like something's missing, but I'm not sure what. Or it's not exactly what I expected, you know? I think I struggle with contentment a little.

Somehow, it feels easy to open up to a stranger on the internet who is across the world from me.

Well, the grass isn't always greener, AJ. I know this.

My husband comes into our bedroom then to check that I'm ready for the walk we'd planned for the afternoon. I find myself wishing I could stay and chat with David longer.

I have to go now, sorry, I say, *we're going for a family walk… hopefully chat soon!*

It was lovely chatting, beautiful AJ! Enjoy your walk :)

A strange, fluttery warmth stirs within me, and I wonder what it means.

***

Later that afternoon, my husband walks into our bedroom and joins me on the bed. It's not unusual for me to lie down for a short nap at this time, but today, instead of resting, my thoughts are going around in circles, contemplating what I should say to him. I know what I need to say – just not the best way to say it.

"Everything alright?" he asks, noticing my uncharacteristic silence. A few more seconds pass before I speak.

"I don't think we're in a good place anymore," I say quietly.

"What do you mean?" he asks, clearly confused.

Silent tears roll down my cheeks as the words spill out of me.

"We don't talk anymore, really talk. I don't know if we ever did. We bicker all the time. The sex is dead, there's no passion, I don't think I'm feeling in love anymore, or in any way I'm supposed to feel… it feels like we're just parents who live together like roommates, it's so platonic. I don't know why it's changed or what to do…"

It's the first time I've articulated all of this – the feelings of dissatisfaction and disappointment, of dullness that have been residing in me for the last few years. It feels good to release it all, but at the same time, I know it's like opening a can of worms. Still, I keep going, unable to stop my verbal barrage. I tell him I need to feel like a woman again, I need to feel he does things to make me feel special, not just like the mother of his child. I want to feel like he loves me properly.

These disclosures, seemingly out of nowhere, appear to have shocked and confused him. But he admits that yes, things have changed.

"I've been feeling the same way, AJ," he admits. "Like things have changed. You haven't made me feel very loved and appreciated either."

"What?!" I ask in disbelief. Now I'm pissed off. I can't believe that instead of just owning it, of taking accountability for how I've been feeling, he would deflect it all back on me like this.

"But you never said you felt like this before! You can't just say that now that I've brought it up."

"There's been so much going on lately," he says. "I haven't had a chance to really think about it. The last few years have been very stressful though; we can try and make it better with us again."

I want to believe him.

After I put our daughter down to sleep that night, I post a couple of new photos on my Instagram, of me posing in our home gym in the garage, next to the exercise bench. I'm wearing tight black bike shorts and my abs are clearly defined beneath my sports bra.

The next morning, I wake to a new message from David in my inbox:

Did you post those photos for me, AJ? When I saw them, my first thought was that I wanted to bend you over that bench and fuck you… You are so sexy, AJ. I hope you don't mind me telling you that.

My heart races and I feel a rush of pleasure; a warm tingle surging through my body. I don't mind it at all.

Raised on a diet of love at first sight and happily ever after, you used to believe in soulmates and destiny, and meeting 'the one'.

You soon grew up, and your library of fairy tales was replaced with textbooks and experts, telling you it was all nothing more than the perfect concoction of chemicals in the brain.

Yes, you know that the euphoria fades, the butterflies vanish.

But is this all you should be left with?

The cynic in you says this is it – it would be the same over and over.

No matter who he was, one day you'd look at him with indifference.

And as you went through the same old motions,

you'd wonder how your heart could trick you again.

Yet something tells you that next time will be different – maybe you know better now; maybe you've learnt what you truly want.

But would following your heart be courageous – or reckless?

Is the grass really not greener?

Or does a whole magical kingdom exist beyond these walls,

waiting to be explored?

CHAPTER 7

Fantasy Lover

My phone light is shining bright.
I'm trying to dim it with the covers,
as I savour each precious moment
that you and I exist as lovers.
Despite the time and space between us,
I feel the two worlds colliding.
Not sure how much more I can do this for,
until I can no longer keep our secret in hiding.
The heat from within me rises,
as your words set my body on fire.
How I long for a time when the stars align,
and I can take in all of your desire.
I quickly check the bed next to me,
to make sure that he's still sleeping.
Then I go back to typing: baby, I need you here,
to feel how hard my heart is beating.

David and I message each other constantly when our awake times align, and our exchanges grow increasingly heated. One Saturday night, as I lie in bed, he describes in detail what he'd do to my body if he were here with me; how he'd touch and kiss me; how he'd make love to me. His words send a rush of excitement through me, making my pulse quicken and my body ache with need. It's like an erotic fiction novel, and I'm the main character.

By the time my husband enters the room, I'm already dripping with desire. As he wraps his arms around me, I reach behind and stroke his cock until it stiffens. I close my eyes, imagining it's David. I picture him thrusting into me, deeper and deeper, as I grind against him.

The next morning, I have some time alone before my daughter and husband wake up. After a shower, I stay in the bathroom, taking photos of my naked body in the mirror to send to David. When my husband and I first met, I didn't have a smartphone with a decent camera, so I never took these kinds of photos for him. I have to admit, it feels thrilling – sexy, naughty, and empowering, all at once.

In one shot, my hand strategically covers one breast, and in another my fingers tease over my pubic area. I imagine David opening my message, his reaction to seeing me like this. The thought sends a jolt of arousal through me. I can't resist the urge to let my fingers slide lower, caressing my pulsating clit. Leaning over the vanity, with one hand on the countertop, I rub myself in a rhythmic motion, trying not to moan too loudly as I bring myself to climax.

Later that day, David tells me my poem has turned him on like crazy, and that if it were possible, he'd be on the next plane over, even if it was just to meet me for a stolen weekend.

Maybe I'll have to steal you, he teases.

Of course, I know it's wrong. I'm a married woman, and I shouldn't even be talking to another man like this, even if just online. But if David were able to somehow come to New Zealand and spend a couple of days with me, how could I resist? I could just say I was going away with my friend again; my husband wouldn't know the difference. I mean, it's not like I'd leave my family for someone who lives in another country, realistically.

David confesses that he's fallen in love with me, and at that moment I feel my heart explode, obliterating all thoughts of reason.

You're so sweet and genuine and beautiful, he says. *It's so unfair there are oceans between us.*

I tell him I love him too. I know when I say it that it's totally illogical. After all, how can I love someone I've never even met? But the feeling of pure bliss that glows inside me when I think of David? It *has* to be love, I think – there's no mistaking it. I share a poem I've just finished with him.

You're my biggest muse lately, I say, hoping he doesn't think it's too much.

> *If you were here in real life,*
> *I think I can picture the way you'd look at me,*
> *the way you'd love me.*
> *Not as your wife or the mother of your child,*
> *but just me – and I'd want to give you it all.*
> *I imagine how it would feel,*
> *your lips on mine, our bodies pressed together.*
> *High on passion, excitement, desire –*
> *all the drugs I've craved for so long.*

I want you to make love to me,
to discover each other completely;
to know all of you and your sweetness.
This distance between us, it tortures yet comforts me,
because how could I restrain myself otherwise?
I still don't know how this happened.
Was I too open to it? Or waiting for it all along?
Either way, you swept me away with your words,
and I let all our feelings wash over me.
I'm drowning in you, but I've never felt so alive.
Looking around me at my life, my reality,
I know it's selfish to contemplate throwing it away,
to even wonder 'what if?'
But you can still stay here, my love,
in my mind and in my heart.

It's so beautiful, David says after he reads it. *You've made me crazy, AJ. I think if I ever come to New Zealand to see you I wouldn't be able to leave – I'd want to stay and be with you always.*

None of it makes sense, we agree. But it all feels so right, so we just go with it.

***

My frustration with the ongoing Covid situation grows. There's talk of the borders opening in the next few months, but even then, quarantine will be required before entering the country. All I want is to meet David, to finally feel his arms around me and his lips on mine. Despite knowing that we won't be together anytime soon, I feel euphoric. I breeze through the days with my head in the clouds.

I go running in the rain, lamenting how amazing and beautiful it is to feel the raindrops dampen my skin. How wonderful it is to *feel* again. *Maybe I'm a little crazy too*, I think. *But, so what?*

> *Amidst my state of numbness,*
> *my residual absence of feeling,*
> *your love for me emerged,*
> *like a tornado.*
>
> *It lifted me up off the ground,*
> *whirled me around,*
> *shook me to life,*
> *and ripped down the walls*
> *around my heart.*
>
> *When it releases me though*
> *I know the fall*
> *will break me.*

One day, after several weeks of our usual, frequent interaction, I send a message to David and, worryingly, twenty-four hours later, he still hasn't replied. I click on his picture beside his message thread to visit his profile, but to my shock, instead of his bio and photos, there's just a message that says: *Sorry, this page isn't available.*

Does this mean David has blocked me? I think, my heart racing with panic. I have no idea what happened; maybe he thought I was too intense with the poem… He was equally intense though, I reason. Or could he have been messing with me just for entertainment? Or was I too distracting for him? How could he do this with no explanation at all?! I've never experienced heartbreak over someone I've never met in person before, but it cuts just as deep.

CHAPTER 8

Come Wandering with Me

I felt like my life was the colour grey before David, but now, in the aftermath of him, I feel black inside. I tell myself it's ridiculous to be so upset, but I can't ignore the hollow feeling within me. I may have had a gnawing sense that something was missing before, but post-David, there's a gaping hole. I try to revert to my status quo as a wife and mother, not someone's object of love and desire, but I can't. It's not enough anymore. It never was, and I cannot go back to pretending. I wonder how I'll fill this void now.

I reflect on how fulfilling it felt – the rush of novelty and passion; wanting and feeling wanted again. How nice it was to have a man be truly interested in getting to know me, desiring me again. It felt good to be seen through fresh eyes, to not be taken for granted. Was I just craving validation? *Maybe*, I think... It had been empowering, though, in a way – turning David on with my photos, seeing and hearing the effect I had on him.

I realise that the intensity of my feelings for David was partly fuelled by *not* having him, by his unavailability. Maybe, if David were here with me all the time, I'd feel no differently about him than I do about my husband, eventually. After all, isn't that where all long-term relationships end up? Passion and being in love aren't sustainable forever, are they?

But then I entertain the idea again: what if David came to New Zealand? What if I ended my marriage to be with him? The thought devastates me – not just for my husband, but for our daughter… I shake my head and blink back tears. I could never do that to her.

What if I don't need to, though? What if I could keep my family together, have the stability and the home base… but also have something more, the extra that I need?

Maybe that's just it, I think. *Maybe our marriage isn't doomed, maybe it's just the rules we've been following need to change.*

Wandering eyes,
they will always stray.
Wandering hearts,
they won't be contained.
Wandering souls;
they need to be free.
I hope you will see that
and come wandering with me.

I don't tell my husband about David, but I do tell him I've been wondering what it would be like to have sex with someone else again.

"Just to experience that passion again, the kind we used to have," I say softly.

He tells me we can get that back; we just need to work on things.

"Like I was saying a few weeks ago, my feelings have changed," I tell him sadly. "I just don't think I'm sexually attracted to you in the way I should be anymore."

His face falls as I continue to speak.

"I don't want to separate or break up our family over this – we have a good life otherwise," I tell him. "But I don't think I can go on like this either."

"What are you saying, AJ? We were going to try and improve things," he says, his voice filled with confusion.

We both fall silent for a few moments, our eyes cast downwards. I take a deep breath and gather my courage to say it, the question I've been dreading: "Would you consider an open marriage?"

"A what?!" His eyes narrow at me in disbelief.

"So that we could stay together as a family but also experience that new, exciting feeling with other people once in a while?"

"What, so you just want to go and sleep around with other guys? No fucking way," he responds, shaking his head abruptly.

Taking no for an answer has never been my strong point, though.

"Is it something you'd be open to if we can work on things between us first?"

He sighs in resignation. "I don't know, AJ. We'd have to be in a much better place to handle something like that."

He tells me we'll be able to get the love back, the passion back again. We just need to read some books on it and find a marriage counsellor. He's always been a practical sort of man.

"Okay, I'll look up someone we can talk to," I say, getting up off the couch.

"But, AJ…" he says as I walk away. I turn to face him.

"If you do decide to just leave, to give up on us without even trying… I won't make it easy for you."

The uncharacteristic threat in his voice disarms me. There's a coldness, a hostility in his eyes I haven't seen before. Maybe it's justified, but I can't help but resent how stifled I feel at that moment.

You just asked your husband if you could sleep with other men – what did you expect?

I want a love that's as invigorating
as raindrops kissing my skin
while I'm running on a drizzly day.

I want a love that's as uplifting
as my favourite music turned up,
sending vibrations
through my soul.

I want a love that's as decadent
as the chocolate left in the box,
so satisfying
that it's the last one I need.

*I want a love that's as stimulating
as the novel I can't put down,
captivating me
as I turn the pages.*

*I want a love that's as assured
as your voice when you tell me
we can have that love again.*

CHAPTER 9

The Girl You Thought You Knew

"I've found a couples' counsellor," I tell my husband later that night. "Her name is Rachel. She has an online booking system, so I've booked us in for Friday at 1pm if that works?"

"Yeah, that should be fine," he says, sitting down beside me on the couch.

"I've also made a few notes about what I think our main issues are," I add. "Maybe you could do the same?"

"What do you mean? Like, my side of things?"

"Yeah, exactly," I say. "You agreed things had changed and said you weren't feeling the same way anymore either. Maybe explain it from your perspective? Just to give some context?"

"Okay, I'll have a think," he replies, and we switch on the David Attenborough documentary we didn't finish the night before.

The following afternoon at work, I check my Gmail account and see an email from my husband. As I read it, his words sting me unexpectedly.

AJ, this is for you to send to the marriage counsellor:

AJ has changed from the happy, relaxed person I married, to someone who is often unhappy and hard to please. She seems to struggle to stay content, even for short periods, and has become overwhelmingly negative most of the time. We've dealt with a lot: financial challenges, the stress of raising a baby, renovations, and, of course, the pandemic, all of which have contributed to these shifts.

In the last four years, things have been especially difficult. For most of those years, we struggled to get any decent sleep due to our daughter waking up often. While AJ was pregnant, I was renovating our house – a doer-upper. After our daughter was born, AJ pushed for us to keep going with the renovations because, according to her, she couldn't live in a half-done house with a baby. Despite my concerns, I agreed to keep moving forward, and it resulted in me working long hours and spending weekends on the house instead of being with AJ and our daughter, which created additional strain.

AJ has always been very single-minded about her goals, often planning ahead without fully considering the present. She'll push for major decisions – like holidays or projects – without always being ready to finish the current one. This has become more intense over the years. If I or anyone disagrees with her, she can be forceful and expects her viewpoint to be accepted, which can lead to conflict.

This contrasts with what she says she wants from me at times, particularly when she says she wants me to have an opinion and contribute to decisions. But when I do, if I disagree, it quickly turns into an argument where I'm accused of being unreasonable or stubborn.

Another issue is that AJ often repeats questions or brings up topics repeatedly, as if the conversation never happened. This has been particularly noticeable with our decision about having a second child. Her views have changed on this repeatedly over the years, sometimes multiple times a day, which has been frustrating for me, especially since I wasn't sure myself.

It feels like AJ often blocks out anything that doesn't fit her current view. She tells me we've never been happy, or that I've never communicated with her. I remember plenty of good times and many conversations we've had, even if I haven't always had the perfect response in the moment.

AJ's negativity seems to stem from focusing on the bad and ignoring the good. Her moods have become unpredictable – one minute we're fine, the next, everything feels wrong. And her anger has escalated, where it now feels like anything can set her off.

In the last few months, AJ has pressed me to 'open up more', but when I do, she accuses me of invalidating her feelings. This has made it difficult for me to feel heard or to communicate my thoughts without fear of a negative reaction. I've tried to express myself in ways that acknowledge her feelings while also sharing mine, but often, it's just not enough.

The combination of her aggression, mood swings, anxiety, and depression has made it hard for me to be the partner she needs. As a result, I've started withdrawing, which I know has likely made things worse, but it has felt like a way to cope.

I return to the spreadsheet I was working on, forcing myself to focus, hoping Kathy in the cubicle across from me doesn't notice my flushed face and tear-filled eyes. Maybe he's right. Maybe everything he said is true. But is it? Am I really that awful? Is it all my fault? Did I make him this way, or was he always like this – and I just didn't see it? Or maybe it's both.

If I'm so bad, why does he still want to try? I know I've had my issues, but maybe this is just his way of deflecting, because he's hurt too. The questions swirl in my mind, faster and faster, until they blur together. I can't make sense of any of it.

> *You wonder where she went,*
> *the carefree girl you knew,*
> *who only had eyes for you.*
> *Her smile and her heart,*
> *once warm and open wide –*
> *isn't it funny that you looked up,*
> *and realised she'd gone,*
> *when you thought she'd be here all along?*
> *Isn't it sad to think you were deceived*
> *by the girl you thought you knew,*
> *the one who slowly disappeared?*

***

With his body facing me on the couch, his knee brushing mine, my husband stares into my eyes. I hold his gaze, but it feels unnatural and I find it hard not to blink. It's supposed to be just two minutes, but it feels like an eternity. Maybe a sign, already, that couples therapy isn't going to work for us.

"You can turn back to me now," Rachel instructs. She asks how it felt.

"It was nice," my husband says, glancing at me with an awkward smile.

"And you, AJ?" Rachel asks, her voice gentle.

I shrug. "I don't know. It felt a bit awkward, I guess."

Rachel's lips tighten, not quite satisfied with our responses. She directs us back to the issues we came to address: my lack of sexual attraction, my spending habits, my anxiety; his stubbornness, spending too much time gaming, lack of motivation, and failure to take more initiative.

"AJ just changed," my husband says, his words flat. "She used to be fun and easy-going. Did you read the background notes she sent you?"

"I had a quick look," Rachel replies. "But I prefer meeting with you both together and hearing it from you directly."

She agrees with him; yes, of course, I've changed. I'm a mother now, with new pressures and responsibilities. We discuss love languages. Mine, I think, is verbal affirmation. My husband's is physical touch, which, according to him, he doesn't get enough of. Rachel suggests my lack of attraction is due to emotional distance, a loss of intimacy.

"When was the last time you held each other when you woke up on Sunday and made love before starting your day?" she asks. I pause. It's been years. Three, at least.

"AJ always gets up before I do," my husband says, the words not quite a defence, but close enough to one. And it's true – I relish the quiet weekend mornings before my husband and daughter wake. At some point, an hour of solitude became more important to me than any desire I had for morning sex.

Morning sex. I recall when I used to lie in bed waiting for my husband to wake up so he could spoon me from behind, and how I'd feel myself get wetter and my nipples stiffen as his morning wood would press into my back. Now I look at him, snoring in bed beside me, unwashed, bad breath… Nothing seems less sexy…

"AJ," Rachel's voice cuts through my thoughts, and I snap back to the present. The small room, the two cream couches facing each other, the powder-blue walls. There's a tiny open window but Rachel's practice is on the third floor of the building so the sounds of the busy street below are muffled and distant. It's supposed to feel peaceful and calm here, but it only serves to remind me how desolate our marriage feels.

"What kind of marriage did your parents have? What did they show you about marriage growing up?" Rachel asks, jotting something in her notebook.

"They fought a lot," I admit. "Not physically, but there were a lot of screaming matches in front of us kids. I never heard them say 'I love you' to each other. My mum talked about divorce, but they stayed together. They're better now, I guess, but they still squabble a lot."

Rachel furrows her brow. "I wonder if because your parents didn't demonstrate to you a loving marriage, if you've idealised what a marriage should look like. Maybe that's something we'll need to work on – a more realistic view of long-term relationships."

"I guess so," I agree, trying to keep my voice steady. "But should all feelings just go completely?"

"No," she says firmly. "Things do change over time. It doesn't have to be a bad thing. It's about adjusting to a different, deeper love. Sometimes, it can even be better than the early stages."

She writes a few scribbled sentences in her notebook again.

In the back of my mind, since the beginning of the session, I've been mulling over whether to broach the subject of open marriages with her. I decide it would be worth hearing Rachel's perspective.

"I've been wondering about open marriages," I say. "It would mean we could stay together and have that committed, deeper love, but also have the novelty and excitement again with other people, is that something you think could work?"

Rachel abruptly stops writing and gives me a pointed look.

"No. I don't believe in open marriages," she says. "You should be getting all your needs met by the same person in a relationship."

Her response is the exact opposite of the one I'd wanted, of course. I glance nervously at my husband, who is staring at Rachel blankly. Hopefully her narrow-minded opinions haven't influenced him too much.

"But what if we can't get any of those feelings back?" I ask worriedly.

"I believe you can," Rachel assures me. "Remember, you're doing this for your daughter. As someone who grew up as an only child with divorced parents, I can tell you; it was *rough*."

"I'm not going back to her," I tell my husband, firmly closing the door to Rachel's practice behind me as we leave.

"She's biased and unprofessional. She has no right to try and make me feel guilty about the only child thing."

He sighs but doesn't disagree. "Find a different counsellor, then."

CHAPTER 10

Redefining the Rules

The following Monday night, after our daughter is tucked up in bed, I settle on the couch and open my laptop. Normally, I'd work on a poem, dive into self-help articles, or watch a show. Tonight, though, I type *open marriages* into the search bar.

Rachel's comment about being an only child with divorced parents has stuck with me since our session on Friday. Sure, I thought she was overstepping by bringing her personal experiences into it, but I can't deny she's probably right. Divorce is hard on any child, but a child without siblings to go through it all with? That feels like a special kind of lonely and traumatic.

The thought has been gnawing at me. All weekend I couldn't stop picturing my daughter being shuffled between two houses. I imagined her in an unfamiliar bedroom, sad and alone, with no one who really understands. What if one of us started a new family? Any additional children would be permanent residents, but she might feel like a temporary guest.

Or what if one of us ended up with someone who already had kids – loud, chaotic kids she'd have to share her space with sometimes? She's just one. They'd outnumber her completely. And if she ever had a step-parent? They could never love her in the same way we did. If my husband wasn't with me, then I'd have no one who could really share my joy and appreciation of raising her and watching her learn and grow in the same way.

We have to stay together for the sake of our daughter, I concluded last night after hours of tossing and turning in bed. There is no other option.

In my mind, opening the marriage is the answer. It would give me the freedom I need without destroying our daughter's life. I just have to figure out how to get my husband on board.

My Google search brings up hundreds of results – articles, Reddit forums, relationship advice websites. Just a quick glance at the first page tells me that open marriages are a polarising topic:

Open marriages have a 92% failure rate.
Open marriages can be just as healthy as monogamous ones.
An open marriage cannot save a marriage.
Open marriages could lower divorce rates.
Open marriages might be happier.

I decide to ignore anything with a negative slant and focus on researching the advantages of open relationships. That's when I stumble upon a term I've never heard before: *ethical non-monogamy*.

Apparently, it's a relationship arrangement where everyone agrees to have multiple romantic or sexual partners, but with clear communication and respect for boundaries. It feels less tacky than the term 'open marriage'; it doesn't give such a seventies free-loving hippie vibe. I like it. I cherry-pick a few articles and email the links to my husband.

When he joins me in the lounge after his gaming session, I ask, "Did you see the email I sent?"

He shakes his head and grabs the TV remote off the coffee table.

"Can we just talk about this for a minute?" I ask, taking it off him.

He sighs and leans back on the couch with his arms behind his head.

"Okay, go on then…" he says, his voice weary.

"I'm not trying to pressure you or anything," I say, "but I did some research. Having an ethically non-monogamous relationship could really help our marriage. It might be just what I need."

He frowns. "What the hell is ethically non-monogamous?"

I explain it to him, feeling like an expert, despite the whole concept being new to me as well.

"It means we set our own rules and boundaries – whatever works for us – and stick to them. It's about being open and honest with each other, so there are no secrets. We could decide if we wanted to be polyamorous, with real relationships on the side, or just keep it casual."

His frown deepens.

"And what if you meet someone and decide you want to leave me for them?"

I sigh. It'd be easier if he'd read the articles first.

"Part of ethical non-monogamy is understanding something called 'new relationship energy'," I clarify for him, making sure to keep my tone calm and reasonable.

"It's that rush of excitement you feel at the start of something new. It's all hormones and chemicals, and it doesn't last. Eventually, any new relationship settles into something more platonic – like what we have now. If we can acknowledge that from the start, whatever we experience with a new person doesn't have to threaten our marriage."

He's quiet for a long moment, his expression unreadable.

"Look," he says, his voice softer now, "I'll read the articles. But you can't expect me to just jump on board right away. It's a massive thing to get my head around."

I'm not good at waiting though.

"Well, I'm glad you're open to it," I say, pushing ahead. "I know it's a big change. But what if we took baby steps? Just started by talking to people online and seeing how it goes?"

"How would we even find people online?" he asks, his tone sceptical.

I shrug. "I don't know. Sometimes randoms on Instagram try to DM me. Or there's Reddit. It seems pretty easy to meet people from overseas."

I think of David then, how we messaged for weeks, the way I exposed my naked body to him, the words I said. A wave of guilt hits me, stabbing at my chest. I remind myself that nothing real was ever going to happen with him. I'd fallen in love with a fantasy, not the real David, whoever he was. I'd been desperately unfulfilled and grasping at anything to feel alive. I promise myself to be honest from now on.

"I just don't see what I'd get out of talking to some random chick online," my husband says, leaning forward again on the couch. He stares down at his clasped hands resting on his lap.

"It could be in a sexual way," I suggest, hoping that will entice him, "and since it's online, it'd be nothing but fantasy – just an escape. No different from watching porn, really."

My husband isn't much of a porn user, but my words get his attention. He sits up straighter and gives me a strange, questioning look that makes me nervous. *Am I not being subtle enough?* I wonder. Is it written all over my face that I've already engaged in a sexually explicit, emotional online affair? I feel my guilt about David deepen then. *Isn't it so manipulative of me*, I think, *to essentially ask to be 'allowed' to cheat after the fact?*

Or maybe my husband is just surprised that despite the sex aversion I've had for the past few years, I'm now interested in getting off to strangers on the internet.

"Maybe," he says, finally, rubbing his temples. "But I still want to read the articles before I agree to anything."

I thank him and feel a surge of cautious optimism. There's hope, at least. We watch a show together but I can't focus, my mind is too busy spinning with new possibilities.

***

The next night, I ask, "Did you have a chance to read the articles?"

He nods. "I can see the logic in it," he says, his voice hesitant. "I guess we can try it for a bit. See if it helps you feel more sexual with me again."

He definitely doesn't share my enthusiasm for the whole venture, but I'm pleased my husband is willing to be uncharacteristically flexible this time. I grin like a kid who just unwrapped the Christmas present they'd been begging for.

"I really think it will help," I reassure him, still not quite believing he's agreed.

"It's online only, though, AJ," he warns. "And no talking to anyone in New Zealand."

"That's fine," I say quickly, thinking of David again, halfway across the world.

"Will it always have to be online?" I can't resist asking.

"I don't know, AJ," he says, sounding more relaxed now. "We'll see how it goes. But don't push it."

I notice a flicker of fear in his eyes as he speaks. Even though I'm excited we're taking steps towards becoming ethically non-monogamous, a small part of me recognises that once we start this, there's no going back. I'm scared too, I realise, but it could be the perfect solution for us, so we need to try it.

"Thank you," I say softly, putting my arm around him as we settle on the couch. "I know it might be weird to adjust to, but there's nothing to worry about."

"I hope not, AJ," he says, offering me a small, uncertain smile.

I was never one to break the rules,
always happy to follow the crowd,
until I realised I didn't like
what I was conforming to.
So, I started to explore
beyond our world of black and white,
and I discovered a place

Redefining the Rules

where we could redefine the rules —
the terms of engagement
to let in a touch of grey,
and a little more freedom.
A place where it's not the marriage,
but monogamy that's the problem.

CHAPTER 11

Alternate Universe

During my spare time over the next couple of weeks, I keep myself occupied by posting some of the poems I've written on my new Instagram account. It doesn't reveal my identity, and it's not linked to any of my personal email accounts, so I'm confident no one I know 'in real life' will come across it.

I give the poems tasteful backgrounds with butterflies and ocean waves, and storm clouds to complement their themes, and I even include photos of myself in some of them. I don't use clear, close-up photos to be safe, but I figure they will give the poems a more authentic, personal touch.

I'm thrilled when I gain a new handful of followers with every post. I've never really put anything out on the internet before like this – it feels rewarding that people are appreciating it and gives me even more motivation to keep writing.

Since my husband agreed to us talking to overseas people online, I haven't had much of a chance to really look into how I'll go about it all. I wonder if there are still chat rooms, like I used as a teenager when my family first got the internet. One night though, there's a new message in my poem Instagram inbox:

Your poems are so beautiful, they really resonate.

I click on the username – it's simply 'Jay' with a long string of letters after it, and the profile image is a half-moon with a dark, ethereal backdrop. *Very mysterious*, I think, my curiosity stirring.

Thank you, I reply. *Who is this?*

The response comes within minutes.

I'm James. Who is the model in your poems? Is that you?

I smile at his flattery, feeling a gush of warmth rise in my chest.

James introduces himself: thirty-eight, living in Dunedin, New Zealand.

I'm in New Zealand too! I type back, surprised.

Wow, that's awesome! Such a small world, he replies, his excitement evident.

I know I'm not supposed to be talking to guys in New Zealand, but Dunedin is nearly at the bottom of the South Island, and I'm close to the top of the North Island. It feels like we're worlds apart. Not much different than talking to someone in Australia, I rationalise.

James admits he's married with three kids but quickly adds that he and his wife are sleeping in separate rooms.

We're probably going to break up, he says.

I tell him how my husband and I aren't in the best place either, but that I'm allowed to talk to people online now for a bit more excitement.

That's really lucky, he says. *My wife would probably kill me if she knew I was talking to you.*

His admission makes me feel like, morally, I should stop talking to him. But then, isn't it really on him, what he's doing behind his wife's back? Plus, he did say they might separate anyway. When I ask, James sends me a photo of himself. He's solidly built with a rugged, slightly unshaven face and short, dark wavy hair. He's wearing a leather jacket, and there's an earring glinting in one ear.

At first glance, he's not my type. But something about his flirtatious, slightly arrogant grin and the twinkle in his blue eyes makes me decide that I am definitely attracted to him.

I ask about his work. He tells me he's mostly a building site manager but also plays in a rock band on the side.

Wanna hear something? James asks, before sending a video clip.

In it, he strums a guitar, singing the opening verses of the song 'Shallow' from *A Star is Born*. His voice is deep, smooth, and unexpectedly soulful.

Just like that, the southern Kiwi tradie transforms into my own Bradley Cooper. And I'm as captivated as Lady Gaga was in the movie.

James says he finds me intriguing and seems eager to get to know me. He's funny in a dry, slightly cocky kind of way and comes across as smart and driven.

Do you have Snapchat? he asks me. I share my username, and he adds me there.

After a few days of chatting, he admits that he isn't actually separating from his wife; they just had a fight, but they're okay now.

The spark's gone, I don't know if we have much of an emotional connection, he says. *I still love her, though, and I could never hurt my family.*

I know exactly how that feels, I reply.

He tells me he connected deeply with the way I describe my feelings on marriage and monogamy in my poems – the 'trapped' feeling, the constant wondering if *this is it.*

I love how your poems seem to come from your subconscious. You're so easy to open up to about these things too, he says. *Normally, I'm a closed book, but you're so kind and genuine, and really wise as well – there's something unique about you.*

I know it's wrong to engage with a married man like this, but I don't resist as James's words pull me in.

You have such beautiful eyes, he responds when I send him a selfie. Before I know it, I'm sending him photos of me in revealing clothes, then lingerie, and eventually, nothing at all.

Oh, God, I want you so bad, he tells me one night as we message in bed.

My husband is still in the bathroom, but for the first time, I don't mind how long he's taking.

James describes how he'd kiss my neck and breasts while running his hands all over my body. His words heat my skin and harden my nipples.

You're making me so, so wet, I tell him.

James confesses that he's masturbating to my photos while his wife sleeps next to him.

She's a deep sleeper, he says. *You make me crazy for you – I can't help myself.*

I'm ashamed that the thought turns me on even more – the idea of a man pleasuring himself over me while his wife sleeps beside him. *There must be something wrong with me*, I think.

I feel kind of bad about that, I tell James. It would be more accurate to say I feel bad because I don't feel bad, though.

You shouldn't feel guilty, James reassures me. *Maybe it was meant to be that we met each other. Maybe this is what we need to be happy – it's like our own alternate universe.*

I slide my fingers into my underwear, submerging them in my arousal.

I want you to fuck me so hard and deep right now, I type with my free hand.

When my husband joins me in bed later, I guide his arm around me and slip off my underwear.

"I think this online chatting stuff is definitely helping," I say, placing his hand over my dripping-wet pussy. The effect is instant – it turns him on so much that for the first time in weeks, he doesn't need the usual efforts from me to get hard.

When we have sex, I close my eyes and imagine that, once again, I'm being fucked by a man I've never met before.

It felt almost like fate when you came across me,
I was searching for something – was it you?
The more we talked, the clearer it became:
you'd been searching for something too.
Something about how you made me smile
made me want to seduce you with my eyes,
and it wasn't long before I found myself wondering
how you'd feel between my thighs.
Now here we are in this alternate universe,

*a place of so many unknowns, so much possibility.
Maybe it's what we've both been seeking all along –
a secret world to explore, just you and me.*

The next few weeks pass by in an exhilarating haze, as James and I keep in constant contact throughout our days at work, and during the evenings. I find myself in a state of perpetual arousal; a constant, subtle vibration running through me. Every message, every photo he sends, is like a jolt of electricity. His vivid descriptions of what he'd do to me send shivers through my body. He's explicit in his desires, sending me videos of himself stroking his cock after I send him sexy photos I've taken for him.

This needs to be inside you, he says one night. *I wish I could have you right this moment.*

But it's not just about the sex. We talk too. About our families, our dreams, our deepest fears and insecurities. James tells me he struggles with anxiety, that the weight of his responsibilities makes him feel like he's never quite enough.

I'm always trying to be a better man, he confesses. *But I always feel like I should be accomplishing more.*

You seem amazing though, I tell him, my heart swelling. *Everything I'd ever want in a partner anyway.*

I ask James if he'd ever seriously considered leaving his wife, seeing he's not happy.

I couldn't, he replies. *The kids need me and we've built too much together to throw it all away.*

Curiosity gets the better of me then, and I ask James if I could see a photo of his wife. He's mentioned how wonderful she is so often that I can't help but want to see the woman who shares his life. He sends me a photo, and I'm struck by how attractive she is. She's tall, slim, and tanned with long brunette hair, and large breasts that peek out of her low-cut white summer dress. She's smiling, flashing perfect white teeth.

I feel a pang of jealousy – it's not that I think I'm less attractive than her necessarily, but I can see why James would've gone for a woman like that. It's hard to understand why he'd be looking for someone else.

She looks lovely, I tell him, my throat tight. *She has way bigger boobs than me, it's not fair, haha.*

James responds almost immediately: *You're my dream woman though.*

Why is that? I ask, a flutter in my chest.

You're beautiful, obviously. But on the inside too. You're kind, sensitive… You're really deep. It just seems like a rare combination. I've never felt this kind of connection with anyone before.

His words dissolve my jealousy almost instantly. I should feel guilty about what we're doing, about the fact that I'm talking to him this way, but in this moment, I feel special. Desired. Something I haven't felt in a long time. It wasn't that my husband had never desired me – of course, he did, especially in those early years when he was head over heels in love with me. But I realise now that he's never had the ability to express it, to articulate all the things he loves about me, not in the way James does. Maybe that's what I've been needing.

I imagine whispered daydreams in my ear,
your most hidden thoughts I've been dying to hear.
Among the shadows together let's play,
in this alternate universe where we're destined to stay.
I close my eyes and pretend it's you I see –
for as long as I think of you, beside me you'll be.

***

One Saturday, I'm on my way back from the supermarket, enjoying the time to myself, even if for something as mundane as grocery shopping. I don't have any reason to rush home to my husband and daughter, so I decide to pull off down a quiet side street and I send James a message:

Are you free for a quick call? I'm just in the car. I can talk for fifteen minutes.

To my relief, he responds immediately.

Okay, that would be great.

James's wife and kids are out, and he's home alone. It's the first time we've video chatted, and it makes everything feel even more real. I'm charmed by his face on the screen, the way his eyes light up when he smiles. He's as confident and funny and easy to talk to as he has been in our text messages. I can't help but feel more drawn to him.

"I've just felt so good since we started this," James says, leaning into the camera with a soft smile. "It's really enhanced my life. I'm so glad we connected."

"Yeah, me too," I admit. "I'm sad we will probably never meet in person though."

James pauses, looking thoughtful.

"You know, it could be possible," he says after a moment. "Sometimes I have to go up to Christchurch for work. Maybe you could fly there one weekend when I'm there, and we could stay in a hotel together…"

I feel my stomach tighten at the thought. The idea of running off for a weekend with James is both exhilarating and terrifying. It feels so out of reach, so impossible… and yet, it seems doable. After all, my husband had been encouraging me to get away more, to do things for myself. A weekend away surely wouldn't raise too many questions from him.

"A weekend in a hotel with you would be amazing," I say, giving him a coy smile. The thought of it feels surreal.

"When do you think you'll be going there next?" I ask, feeling a rush of anticipation.

CHAPTER 12

Unchained

A few nights later, James tells me he could arrange to be in Christchurch in three weeks.

I'll sort the hotel, he says. *You just need to get there. Hopefully, flights won't cost you too much.*

I quickly check online – there are specials flying from where I live to Christchurch; it would only be a two hundred dollar round trip.

Yeah, the flights aren't too bad actually, I tell James. *I'll just need to check with my husband to make sure it's okay for me to go away that weekend.*

Despite my confidence that I could get away with saying I'm going away with my friend, I'm plagued with anxiety and guilt. If my husband found out the truth – that I'm sneaking off to meet someone – it would be the end of everything.

I know James is who he says he is, and I trust my intuition that I'll be safe with him. But what if something went wrong? What if I had an accident in Christchurch, and my husband found out I wasn't with my friend at all? My mind continues to spin with hypothetical worst-case scenarios. After a while, I realise there's no way I can lie to my husband about who I'm meeting. I can't book those flights. There must be another way.

"Have you met anyone online to talk to yet?" I ask my husband that night when he joins me on the couch.

"Yeah, I've chatted to a couple of girls in the UK through one of my gaming forums," he says. "But nothing's really stuck. It seems a bit pointless, to be honest. Have you?" he asks, tilting his head toward me.

I glance down at my hands, my thumb catching my attention. There's a broken piece of skin near the nail, and I start peeling it back slowly. A tiny bead of blood rises to the surface, but I don't stop.

"You need to stop that," my husband scolds, tapping my wrist firmly. His tone is sharp, like a parent catching their child in a bad habit.

I try to hold still, my mind racing as I prepare myself to confess.

"I have been talking to one guy on Instagram," I say, trying to sound casual about it.

"Oh?" my husband asks, his interest piqued. "Where does he live?"

I take a deep breath. "Well, that's the issue. I didn't find out until we'd been chatting for a while that he actually lives in Dunedin."

My husband's eyes narrow, his jaw tightening. "Well, you can't talk to him then," he says, his tone resolute. "That's what we agreed – overseas only."

"I haven't been able to meet anyone overseas," I tell him, my cheeks beginning to flush. "And it's not like I can just drive all the way to Dunedin to see him."

My husband sighs, rolling his eyes. He's annoyed, understandably, but I decide to push on with what I'd been thinking about asking him regardless.

"It has been really helping, talking to him online," I explain. "It's exciting and fun, and it gives me an escape from this everyday version of myself. And you know it's made a difference to our sex life."

My husband nods slowly, his face softening a little. "Yeah, I've noticed that. It's helped you feel more sexual again, I guess."

"I don't think it's going to be fulfilling to keep having only online connections though," I add. "Would you consider us being able to actually meet people who live in different cities, like once every couple of months?"

I hold my breath, waiting for his response.

"I just don't know if I could handle the idea of some other guy fucking you," he says finally, staring at the floor.

"I know it won't be easy," I reply, my voice steady. "But it should be manageable. Did you read about *compersion* in that ethical non-monogamy stuff I sent you?"

He shrugs. "Yeah, a little. I can't really remember, though."

"It just means we can learn to be happy for each other when we experience pleasure with someone else," I explain.

I think back to the early years of our relationship when I would get consumed with jealousy just seeing him look at another woman. I try to picture him with someone else

– kissing her, entwined with her, making love to her. I pay attention to my body's reaction. Nothing. It depresses me a little, but at the same time, it's liberating.

"I think I could be okay with you being with someone else," I tell him. "It would be like having consensual affairs – an escape from normal life, but the people we meet would live far away, and it would only be maybe once every couple of months. It wouldn't affect our marriage or family life."

I know I'm being a little naive, and that opening our marriage to this extent could have far greater implications than I've really considered. But I'm certain it's the right choice for us.

"I just don't think I'm a naturally monogamous person," I say firmly. "Some people just aren't."

My husband sighs again, putting his feet up on the coffee table.

"I still don't know, AJ," he says, his voice tense. "I'm not completely opposed to it, though. So, if you really want this, you need to make a contract. Write out all the rules. And I'm still not saying I'll agree to it, but I'll think about it."

***

The next night, after putting our daughter to bed, I open a new Word document on my laptop. My thoughts have been racing all day, excitedly anticipating this. *Open Marriage Rules* I name the file before clicking the save button. After several rewrites, I finally come up with a list of rules that sound clear, logical and unambiguous enough for there to be a chance my husband will agree to them.

Open Marriage Rules

1. *We can engage with other people we meet on dating apps, but they must not be local and must be based at least three hours' driving distance away from us.*
2. *We have the option to meet someone in person no more than* once *within a two-month period. This can be an overnight date and include sex.*
3. *We must communicate regularly about who we're talking to and planning to meet, and provide details about the person and hotel name prior to meeting for safety reasons.*
4. *Communication with others must not overtake time with our daughter, family activities, or time we would normally spend together, such as watching TV/movies at night.*
5. *Condoms must be used during sex with other people.*
6. *We must continue to work on improving our own sex life and relationship.*
7. *We will not disclose our ethically non-monogamous lifestyle to anyone we know in real life for privacy reasons.*

"Have a look at these," I tell my husband, thrusting my laptop onto his lap as he sits down on the couch later. I hold my breath and I wait for him to read over the contract.

"These are pretty reasonable," he says after a couple of minutes.

I'm relieved by his positive reaction – I'd been nervous the 'rules' would make everything feel too real and that he'd backtrack on the whole idea. I can't believe we're actually doing this. It feels like our stale, dull marriage has been hit with a ray of sunshine; given a new lease of life.

My earlier fears about introducing other people to our relationship have evaporated, I realise; all I can think about is the possibility of meeting James now.

Maybe that was the problem all along – I've been trying to find happiness in a monogamous relationship, when it turns out I'm just not cut out to be monogamous. Of course I'd naturally feel trapped with one person when I have the capacity and need to desire, and even love, other people.

"This should work out really well," I assure my husband.

They slipped through her fingers,
those old, tired chains
untethered at last;
she'd set herself free.
And although the fantasy of escape
still rushed through her veins,
she realised it was just as good
to now have the option
to come and go as she pleased.

CHAPTER 13

Black Hole

I have some great news, I message James the next day during my lunch break. I wait impatiently for fifteen minutes before he finally opens the message and replies.

What is it, sexy?

Smiling, I quickly type back, explaining the details about my open marriage contract.

So now I'm allowed to fly to Christchurch to meet you, and I won't have to lie to my husband about anything!

James reads the message. I see the *James is typing…* notification pop up, then disappear, then reappear again. My stomach tightens as the seconds drag on. What's taking him so long? Surely, he'd be as excited about this as I am.

Finally, a reply appears.

I guess that's good… Tbh, I think I liked it when it was just us that knew about this. It felt more special, like we were secret lovers. Now it's riskier too – what if your husband tells my wife?

The last thing I expected was any reservation from him. For a moment, I just stare at the message, feeling a pang of disappointment.

My husband would never do that, I reply, my fingers moving quickly over the keys. *He's not that kind of person… and he doesn't know you're married either.*

It's true. My husband has the highest integrity of anyone I've ever met; he'd never condone me seeing someone who was married. I try to reassure myself that it's not *my* problem James is married, that this is his decision, his responsibility. Still, a flicker of guilt nags at me.

Do you not want to meet me anymore? I say, the words heavy with unease. Has he changed his mind completely?

Of course I still want to meet you, James responds, and I exhale in relief.

Go ahead and book the flights for the weekend after this one. I've already told my wife I'll need to be in Christchurch for work, and she's fine with it.

That night, I book my flights. My heart pounds as I enter my credit card details and confirm the payment. Non-refundable. *There's no turning back now*, I think, as I stare at the confirmation email. This is really happening.

A part of me wonders if I'm being driven by some kind of temporary insanity. It's so out of character for me to do something like this. But then I think of James – his smile, his laugh, the way he makes me feel alive. I want him so badly in person that my doubts are easy to brush aside.

I let my mind wander to how it will feel when we finally meet. I picture stepping off the plane and seeing him for the first time – his arms wrapping around me, his lips brushing mine, the heat of his touch. We'd go somewhere intimate for dinner and drinks, unable to keep our eyes or hands off each other.

My breath quickens as I imagine him undressing me later, his hands exploring every inch of my body, the magnetic pull of weeks of tension finally releasing as he moves against me. A tremble runs through me, leaving a throbbing ache between my thighs. *It's going to be perfect*, I tell myself. *It has to be.*

> *You're the rip tide in the ocean;*
> *I tell myself I'll drown*
> *if I try to swim against it.*
> *And so, I find myself drifting –*
> *deeper, deeper.*
> *You're the fire in the darkness;*
> *and I'm the moth.*
> *I tell myself it's instinctual*
> *as I'm drawn to your flames.*
> *You're the edge of the cliff,*
> *and I'm running towards you –*
> *faster, faster.*
> *I tell myself it's too late to stop,*
> *and let myself fall.*

I send James a message to let him know I've booked the flights.

I can't wait to do all the things to you I've been fantasising about for so long, he tells me.

Me neither! I reply.

We chat intermittently throughout the weekend as usual, but come Monday morning, my 'goodnight' message from Sunday night is still showing as 'delivered' on Snapchat. In the office, I try to focus on my work, but there's a gnawing feeling in my stomach. I can't stop checking my phone every ten minutes, hoping James will open my message. By 2.45pm when it's time to leave, he still hasn't. I try not to get too anxious – he did say he's been really busy with work lately. But it's just not like him to leave my messages unread.

It's 9pm that night when James finally sees my message and replies:

I'm sorry for going silent, he says. *My wife asked to check my phone. She's acting really suspicious.*

His words send a flicker of unease through me. This is the last thing we need. James tells me he's hidden his Snapchat in a folder so she wouldn't find our messages, but she did go through his Instagram and made him unfollow all the random women he'd been following, including my poems page.

She's acting weird, he says. *Really clingy, checking up on me constantly, even saying she wants to come to Christchurch with me.*

My heart sinks.

So, you'll have to cancel meeting me then? I ask, preparing for the worst.

Not necessarily, he replies. *I've told her it's just a boring work trip and there's no reason for her to come. We'd have to figure out leaving the kids with her parents too.*

I don't feel very optimistic about it all, though.

Don't worry too much yet, he says, as if sensing my worry. *I'll sort it out. Hopefully she'll feel more secure by then.*

I don't hear from James again until three days later, when I'm about to get into bed.

Hey, babe, James says. Then he sends me a photo – a

selfie he's taken, and I can see by the background that he's at the gym. He isn't smiling and his face is glistening with sweat.

I glance at the time on my phone: it's 10.20pm.

You're at the gym at this time? I ask.

Yeah, he replies. *I've felt really stressed all day. Just had to get out of the house.*

Then he tells me his wife has agreed to stay home while he's in Christchurch. I'm relieved, but something about the tension in James's face and the unusual lateness of him going to the gym unsettles me.

I can't wait to do all the things to you I've been fantasising about, he says. *Talk to you soon.*

I can't wait either, I say. *Hope you feel better tomorrow x.*

He doesn't open that message, though. For the rest of the week, I obsessively check my phone. But when Saturday rolls around, I still see the 'delivered' status on my message. It's exactly one week before my Christchurch trip.

***

On Monday at work, I can barely focus. In frustration, I put my phone on silent and toss it into my bag, vowing to check it only every two hours. By the end of the day, the message is still sitting on 'delivered', with no change. I feel helpless, unsure of what to do. I even try calling James on Snapchat, but he doesn't answer.

"I don't know what to do," I cry to my husband as soon as he walks through the door.

Our daughter is settled on the couch, watching *Peppa*

Pig. I've been too frazzled since I got home to even think about what to cook for dinner.

"Why, what's wrong?" he asks, kicking off his shoes.

"It's the guy I'm supposed to see this weekend; he hasn't even been in touch since last week," I say, my voice shrill and panicky.

My husband looks at me, shrugging. "I dunno, maybe he's busy."

I sigh, my frustration at the situation growing. I realise it's not my husband's responsibility to listen to me vent about another guy seemingly ghosting me. I don't say anything further.

Later that night, instead of writing or doing anything at all while my husband is gaming, I sit on our bed, staring at my phone. To my surprise, after five minutes, I receive a notification that James has sent a message. My hands shake as I unlock my phone and open Snapchat. It's an unusually lengthy message, and as I read it, my chest burns, and hot tears spring to my eyes.

I'm sorry, AJ. I can't do this anymore. I've been at the doctor's all day after having an anxiety attack, it's too much. It's gotten too real now, and I care about my family too much. I can't hurt them. Please know that I didn't mean to mess you around. I'm so sorry.

I read the words again, my brain trying to process what he's saying. An anxiety attack? Was the idea of cheating actually making him feel that bad? I'd had no idea… I feel very ashamed of myself suddenly. *I shouldn't have tried to pursue anything with a married man*, I scold myself, *it was selfish and wrong.*

Finally, I get myself together enough to formulate a response.

Please don't be sorry, I begin, but as I'm typing, the entire chat vanishes.

I check Instagram – his profile is gone there too, it's as if he never existed. I don't know his last name. I google 'James' with the city he lives in, his job… but there are no results.

My husband walks into the bedroom to find me lying on the bed, face buried in the pillow.

"What's wrong?" he asks.

"I'm not going to Christchurch anymore," I sob. "That guy I was supposed to meet… he just told me he's married and he freaked out." The lie spills from my mouth, dripping with emotion so convincing that even I can almost believe it. I know I should tell him the truth, but then he'd be so angry, so disappointed in me.

My husband looks shocked. "What an arsehole," he says. "That's shit for you – but at least you found out now." He holds me in his arms until I stop crying and my body relaxes.

How fucked up this is, that my husband is comforting me because I'm upset that a man couldn't bring himself to physically cheat on his wife with me. *Maybe I'm getting what I deserve*, I think.

I vow to myself that, going forwards, I will actually practise ethical non-monogamy ethically. I will be open, honest, and transparent with my husband, and I will not be complicit in affairs. Hopefully tomorrow I won't feel so sad about James, either.

"Maybe tomorrow I'll try a dating app," I tell my husband, sitting up and wiping away my tears.

*The day before yesterday cut
like a knife through my core.
The pain so raw.
You left my heart reeling.
Yesterday dried up my tears
and though inside was sore
it didn't hurt like before.
I could feel myself healing.
Today left me with a scar;
the wound's not there anymore.
Maybe tomorrow will close the door
and I'll think of you without feeling.*

CHAPTER 14

The Pleasures We Live For

I remember a couple of years after I met my husband, after we drunkenly bumped into each other and started dancing together at a nightclub, Tinder was born. For anyone, like me, who settled down prior to the era of dating apps, it certainly felt like we had missed out on all the options and convenience they provided. The idea of swiping through hundreds of people, chatting, flirting, and setting up dates from the comfort of your own home seemed so alluring. I couldn't help but feel a little sense of missing out. I wonder, *would I have swiped right on my husband if I'd seen him on there?* I decide I probably would have. My husband is one of those people who look better in photos than in person though – maybe I'd have turned up to a date with him and been disappointed.

When I download Tinder, I quickly realise it only allows me to set my location to where I actually am. That means anyone I know here who happens to be on the app would see me. I search for alternatives and find another dating app, Badoo, which allows manual location settings. Perfect. I set mine to Christchurch. It's far enough away and happens to be where I'd already planned to go to meet James. As it turns out, Air New Zealand has a special cancellation policy for during Covid, which meant I could put my cancelled flights in credit instead of losing the money. At least I wasn't out two hundred dollars on top of everything else.

Scrolling through my phone's gallery, I select several of the most flattering photos of myself. Filling out the basic details for my Badoo profile is straightforward: height, education, religious beliefs, and so on. The bio, however, requires more thought. I need to be honest about being married and limited in terms of time, but I also don't want to attract men who are only looking for a one-night stand. Emotional connection is still important to me. After some deliberation, I write:

Happily married mum of one exploring ethical non-monogamy. Looking for fun, casual connections with interesting, open-minded people.

I save my changes. My profile is live.

Before I even start swiping through profiles, the notifications come flooding in. Likes. Chat requests. More likes. I click on a few profiles of the men who have already liked me. Some are decent, but most are… well, not for me. The dating app clichés are all true: men holding fish, men looking much older than their listed age, and selfies that resemble mugshots more than portraits. But among them are a few who catch my eye – professional, fit, well groomed, outdoorsy, and with bios that display proper spelling and grammar.

Within fifteen minutes, I've accumulated ten matches, and a few have already sent messages.

Hey, there, one says.

Hey! I reply, feeling a small thrill of excitement. *How's your night going?*

But he ignores my question and cuts straight to the chase.

I just read your bio. Does your husband know you're on here?

Yes, he does, I reply.

That's a first! he responds, with a laughing emoji.

I go on to explain my situation. *He does know I'm on here. We're trying an open marriage and are allowed to meet people every couple of months. All good if that's not your thing though…*

He doesn't reply for a few moments.

Hmm… he finally says. *To be honest, it's not really. There's no way I'd be letting my missus meet up with other men. All the best to you and your husband, though.*

And with that, he un-matches me.

The judgment stings more than I expect, but I remind myself that not everyone will understand or approve of my situation.

Thankfully, the next couple of guys I chat with are more open-minded.

My ex and I tried an open relationship for a bit, one says.

Do you and your husband have threesomes together? he asks after a few exchanges.

The question makes me pause. I try to visualise my husband and me in a threesome. I've never felt a desire to sexually experiment with another woman, so it would have to involve my husband and another man. But the thought feels… wrong. As if he doesn't belong in any of the hot, kinky scenarios I've fantasised about. The idea of him watching me with another man only makes me think about how emasculating it might feel for him. The entire concept leaves me cold.

No, we're just doing things separately, I reply.

We chat a little more, and I reveal that I don't actually live in Christchurch but would be able to come down every couple of months.

I'm probably looking for something a bit more regular than that, sorry, he responds.

I un-match him as well and resume swiping until my husband comes into the lounge.

"You ready to watch something?" he asks, grabbing the remote control from under a cushion.

"Yeah, in just a moment," I say, my eyes glued to my phone. "I joined Badoo tonight. It's kind of fun. It's going to be hard to meet someone in another town, though."

He glances over my shoulder at the screen, watching curiously as I swipe and scroll through profiles, notifications, and messages.

"You're like a kid in a candy store," he says drily, a bemused smile tugging at the corners of his mouth.

***

After a week of seemingly endless conversations on Badoo that have gone nowhere, I match with Dane. He's thirty-seven, 172cm (kind of short, I note), lives in Christchurch, and has short brown hair and brown eyes. He's slim built, and his selected interests say he's into the gym and running.

Not really sure what I'm looking for here, but open to chats and dates and seeing if we click… then let's see where it goes :)

I like that his bio makes him seem down to earth, modest, unassuming, and approachable. *Maybe he won't mind that I'm married*, I think hopefully. I send the first message.

Hey, Dane! Nice to match. How are you tonight?

His reply comes through in a matter of seconds.

Hey, AJ! You too :) I am very well this evening, thank you, and yourself? You look stunning in your photos, by the way.

I smile to myself. Finally, someone on here who is respectful and compliments me nicely without being overtly sexual or gross about it. I decide to be upfront with Dane straight away.

I'm great, thanks, just another Tuesday night! And thank you! You look nice in yours too. I should tell you, I don't actually live in Christchurch, I'm closer to Auckland, actually. My husband and I are new to this ENM thing, though, and want to be discreet.

Oh, okay. How does that work, though? he asks. *Are you just here to chat to people?*

No, I explain. *I guess I'm hoping to find someone I really click with who would be open to seeing me every couple of months – we have some rules for our open marriage, so that's how often I'd be able to come down there. Would something like that work for you?*

I bite my lip, hoping Dane's response will be more favourable than the others so far.

Well, it's not ideal, he says. *But I'm pretty open to anything, really. I've been single for about a year now and not having much luck finding something serious again. It would be nice to have someone to talk to and catch up with sometimes.*

Dane's response is exactly what I'd hoped to hear. For the first time since starting this, I feel like maybe this whole idea of finding someone new might actually work.

That's great! I reply.

We keep chatting for the next hour. He tells me he's a team leader at some kind of warehouse. He's lived in Christchurch all his life and hasn't travelled anywhere except the Gold Coast in Australia once as a teenager.

Not educated and not well travelled, I critique him inwardly, mentally ticking through my checklist. Maybe I'm being a bit picky, though – *AJ, you're just looking for a side guy, not a fricken new husband, for God's sake*, I tell myself.

Dane asks me about my husband and my daughter.

She's almost five. We decided to be one and done…

Can I just ask about your marriage? he asks after a pause, catching me slightly off guard.

Sure, anything you want to know?

I can't get my head around the whole 'open marriage' thing – what made you decide to try it?

Resting my phone on my lap, I sit back on the couch, staring blankly at some reality show playing on the TV as I consider my response.

I guess, after a few years, our relationship started to feel really platonic – kind of lost the spark, I explain. *He's a good husband overall, though, and we don't want to separate or anything for the sake of our daughter. So just trying this so we can experience that feeling of novelty and excitement and attraction again with other people, without it affecting our lives too much.*

That makes sense, Dane replies, seeming to accept my explanation.

Soon after, he tells me he needs to get to bed as he has an early start.

You seem really lovely; it's been nice getting to know you. Hopefully, we can chat again soon.

Yeah, definitely keen, I tell him.

Before wishing him goodnight, I give him my Snapchat username. Maybe Dane isn't my 'dream guy', but he's kind of cute, and seems very trustworthy and genuine so far. I'm cautiously hopeful about where this connection with him might lead.

It's not the secrets we keep,
nor the desires we hide.
Not the dreams forgotten.
Or the pleasures denied.
It's the secrets we share,
the desires we don't ignore.
The moments we create,
the pleasure we live for.

CHAPTER 15

What Am I Searching For?

Early on Saturday morning, two weeks later, I'm packing my suitcase.

"Are you sure you're okay with this?" I ask my husband as I rummage through my underwear drawer, searching for my sexiest lingerie.

We'd discussed it last week before I booked the flights to meet Dane in Christchurch. My husband's main concern was my safety – he wanted Dane's full name, the time I'd arrive, and the name of the hotel Dane had booked for the night.

"We've video chatted a few times," I'd reassured him. "He's a really nice guy. No red flags or anything."

My husband looks up, still half asleep. "Yes, AJ. I told you, it's all fine," he says, rubbing his eyes.

Later that morning, my husband pulls into the drop-off zone at the airport.

"Make sure you text me as soon as you get there and meet him," he says.

"I will," I promise.

Before grabbing my suitcase, I open the back door and lean in to hug my daughter in her car seat.

"Where are you going again, Mummy?" she asks, clutching my shoulders.

"To Christchurch to see a friend, remember?!" I say brightly, trying to force down the lump forming in my throat.

"Make sure you're good for Dad, okay? I love you."

"I love you, Mummy. Bye!" she says, as I kiss her one last time and shut the door. I wave at my husband, trying to ignore the tiny voice in my head screaming, *what are you doing?! This is fucking crazy.*

Inside the airport, I check in and have thirty minutes to calm my nerves before boarding. Less than two hours later, I'm in Christchurch. My eyes scan the crowd in the Arrivals area. As soon as I spot Dane, my heart sinks. He's shorter than I expected, probably only two inches taller than me, and his scrawny frame seems almost swallowed by his black hoodie and ripped jeans. He looks like the same person as in his photos and our video calls – just a lot smaller, and with his demeanour and fine features, he comes off as a bit ratty almost. It makes me realise then how deceiving cameras can be – either that, or Dane shares my husband's misfortune of not transposing well to a three-dimensional context.

He hasn't seen me yet. Should I just turn around and book the next flight home? Could I come up with an excuse? My mind whirls with escape plans until Dane glances up from his phone. His face lights up with a shy grin as our eyes meet. *Stay calm. Suck it up for now*, I tell myself, forcing a warm smile.

"Hey, AJ!" Dane says, walking over. "You look great."

"Hey! Thanks, nice to meet you!" I exclaim. We share an awkward embrace, and he offers to take my suitcase.

As we walk through the parking lot, I force myself to make small talk, even as my nerves tighten.

"This is me," he says, gesturing toward a navy-blue Falcon. I climb into the passenger seat, and seconds later, we're off.

"You feeling okay?" Dane asks as he slows for a red light. He's leaned forward, tightly gripping the steering wheel; he looks a little tense as well.

"Yeah, a bit nervous, but I'm all good," I tell him, trying to shake off my unease.

I'm here now, I text my husband as Dane pulls into the underground car park of a hotel near the CBD.

He seems nice so far, I add. *Pretty sure he's not a serial killer, haha. Think it should go fine!*

***

That evening, after I've freshened up, Dane and I head to a rooftop bar downtown. I've brought a little black dress and pointy heels for our night out together, but even though Dane has changed into a streamlined dark-grey shirt, I feel overdressed next to him.

Our conversation starts off a little strained – Dane's pleasant enough but he doesn't seem to have a lot of depth.

Maybe he's just a bit shy though, I think. I ask him a lot of questions about himself and the awkwardness starts to ease, fortunately. By my second glass of Pinot Gris, I feel a warm, fuzzy buzz that thankfully makes Dane seem more appealing. *He's pretty cute actually*, I observe through my beer goggles.

He shifts closer in the booth and rests a hand on my knee. An unexpected tingle shoots up my leg. Even though I'm not wildly attracted to Dane, part of me wants him to touch me more.

"I just wanted to say, AJ," he says, looking into my eyes, "I was so keen to meet you, and you're such a babe in person too."

"Thank you," I reply, pleased the alcohol has obviously given him some confidence. "You're really nice – I'm glad I chose you to be the first guy I meet in this open marriage thing."

After drinks, we head to a sports bar for dinner. Not many restaurants had free tables, so we settle for platters and another round of drinks.

When Dane asks if I'm ready to head back to the hotel, I hesitate for just a second before saying, "Sure."

He slings his arm around my waist as we walk, at one point pinching my arse with his fingers. I laugh it off, but it's a forced laugh. It makes me feel cheap, objectified – like I'm an escort he's hired for the night.

That's what I essentially am, isn't it? Just no-strings sex – except I didn't even cost more than a few drinks and a pub meal. I push these thoughts away and focus on enjoying the night.

Once back at the hotel, still tipsy, I sit on the edge of the bed and remove my heels. Dane sits beside me and takes my face in his hands, leaning in to kiss me. His lips are soft, and for the first time in years, kissing feels exciting – like it's building up to something more.

I lie back and pull Dane on top of me, our limbs tangled. It feels new and illicit, and I let myself get lost in the thrill of being with someone who isn't my husband for the first time in years. *I can't believe I'm actually doing this*, I think excitedly.

But as things progress, the mood shifts. Dane's hands are rough, almost clumsy, and when I guide him inside me, he slips out immediately. We try again. And again. Each attempt ends the same way.

"I'm really sorry," Dane apologises, collapsing back onto the pillows. "I should've told you earlier… I had an accident during sex a few years ago. A girl was on top of me, going hard, and I felt something snap, and now…"

I stare at him, unsure what to say. "Oh my god! Did you see a doctor?"

"Yeah, but I waited too long," he says sadly. "They said if I'd gone right away, before the fracture healed up, they could've fixed it. Now I'm half the size I was. It really knocked my confidence."

I nod, not knowing how to respond.

Dane grins then, a little sheepishly. "Lucky I'm really good with my hands, though, right?"

I let him try for a few more minutes, but there's only so much of his rough fondling I can take. Eventually, I decide the kindest thing to do is fake an orgasm.

"Did you come?" Dane asks, after I've finished moaning and writhing my body in feigned pleasure.

"Yeah," I say, breathing hard still, "that felt so good!"

I nudge Dane onto his back and then go down on him until he finishes in my mouth, thankfully it doesn't take long.

Dane spoons me from behind and caresses my body for a few minutes before he drifts off to sleep. I roll away from him and close my eyes, wishing I could just be here alone now.

***

"I had a really good night," Dane says as he pulls into the drop-off zone at the airport the next morning. We'd had a quick brunch together before leaving, but conversation had felt stilted, weighed down by the awkwardness of the previous night.

"Hopefully you can come back in another two months?" he asks, turning to me with a hopeful smile.

"Yeah, it was a nice night," I say, offering a quick hug before grabbing my suitcase. "We'll keep in touch, and maybe I can arrange another trip sometime."

But as I walk into the terminal, I know I'm just being polite. Now that I'm sober, and with the memory of last night's disappointing sex still fresh, I have absolutely no desire to see Dane again.

***

"How was it?" my husband asks once I'm back home later that afternoon. We're careful to wait until we're out of earshot of our daughter.

"It was fun," I say, unsure how to articulate my mixed emotions. "It was nothing to write home about though, to be honest. I think it's too risky for me to just fly somewhere to meet someone like that. If I could meet people in Auckland instead, I could at least go on a date first, then decide if I want to commit to a night in a hotel."

My husband's face hardens. He throws up his hands. "Auckland's only a ninety-minute drive from here, AJ. That's way too close!"

"I think it's reasonable," I argue, my voice rising slightly. "It'd just be for a quick coffee or something. We could allow one day trip every two months for that. Then, if we get along with the person, we could arrange the sleepover thing for the second meeting, still only once every two months. There wouldn't need to be two months between the initial meeting and the overnight date though, of course," I add, wanting to ensure I'm covering my bases.

He folds his arms across his chest, glaring at me in silence for several moments.

"Fine," he says finally, his tone clipped. "Rewrite that into the contract then. But you need to stop pushing for more – it's always something with you."

I nod, satisfied that I've managed to renegotiate the rules to better suit me. I immediately change my location on Badoo from Christchurch to Auckland – meeting men in Auckland will make things much easier. But as I unpack my suitcase later, I can't shake the emptiness creeping over me. The weekend with Dane has left me unsettled, hollow.

I need to get it right next time, I think.

Moments of smiles, moments of tears;
transient feelings fill my empty heart.
The outside appears perfectly together,
yet the structures are cracking apart.
Moments of euphoria, moments of nothing;
delusional dreams blur with reality.
My perception of life through distorted lens –
it never quite measures up to fantasy.
Moments of clarity, moments of indecision,
ever-changing sides in this internal war.
No permanence of thoughts or emotions;
just the resounding question: What am I searching for?

CHAPTER 16

Love Is My Drug

Lately, I've noticed my husband is on his phone a lot, texting. There's a glint in his eye and a sheepish smile on his face that's at odds with the man I've been living with in recent years.

"Have you found anyone off the apps yet?" I ask casually, as I jot down items for the grocery list.

"Can you put down a new aftershave?" he asks, pouring himself a glass of water.

"Sure. So, have you found anyone yet?" I ask again.

He takes a long drink and nods. "Yeah, I'm talking to someone," he admits. "A woman in Auckland. She's in a loveless and sexless marriage, apparently – married her husband for visa reasons. They're not separating because of their kids, but they've agreed they can meet other people."

I stop writing and glance up. "Do you think you'll meet her in person?"

He shrugs, looking slightly uncomfortable. "I don't know if I'm ready for that. Maybe one day."

His response bothers me, though I'm not sure why. Maybe it feels unbalanced – that I've already slept with someone, and he hasn't. Or maybe it's because this lack of initiative, this passivity, is so typically him. I remind myself I should feel relieved – if he's supposedly fine with me seeing other people, but isn't diving into it himself, that's a win, right? It would make our marriage easier to maintain.

He picks up his phone again and chuckles at it, a quiet laugh that's almost boyish. It's disconcerting, seeing this version of him – a version I'm not part of.

"What's funny?" I ask, forcing my tone to stay light.

"Oh, Sarah just sent me a meme," he says, grinning. "She has exactly my sense of humour, such a crack-up."

"Good you've met someone," I say, my lips tightening into a polite smile. I don't want to let on that I'm unsettled by how light-hearted and jovial he is talking to this 'Sarah'.

I return my focus to the grocery list, trying to ignore the twist in my stomach. He deserves to feel this – this spark, this connection – but it's jarring to see it from the other side. I tell myself I have no right to feel this way. After all, he's been watching me do the exact same thing for weeks now.

At the supermarket, I carefully choose a nice, thick cut of Scotch fillet to have for dinner tonight.

"Look at the price of it, AJ!" my husband snaps, grabbing the tray off from me before I can put it in the trolley. "Almost $50 a kilo! Get a cheaper steak."

"I love Scotch fillet though, it's not that much," I tell him. "Plus, I don't like cheap steak."

"AJ, we're not getting that, you're being ridiculous," he scolds me, and switches it for a tray of limp, dry-looking rump steak that's half the price.

I notice a couple of people in the meat section glance our way. With my cheeks burning, I swiftly push the trolley with our daughter in the front down one of the aisles. It's not about the steak, of course, but rather being made to feel small, as if he's trying to exert power over me – something I've caught him doing a few times lately.

"Please don't ever talk to me like that again," I warn my husband once we're out the supermarket and loading grocery bags in the boot.

"What do you mean?" he asks, as if he's forgotten the incident already.

"Like I'm a child!" I exclaim. "It was condescending, and embarrassing, especially in public, and you shouldn't teach our daughter that it's acceptable for a woman to be spoken to that way!"

He rolls his eyes and mutters something inaudible under his breath.

A heavy silence fills the air on the drive home. *Is this what our relationship has become?* I wonder. Quiet resentments bubbling under the surface, brought to boiling point by something as innocuous as a Scotch fillet?

***

The next morning, I drive to Auckland to meet Ryan, a guy from Badoo I've been chatting to for the past couple of weeks. Ryan is thirty-five, British, and has some kind of analyst job. He told me he's recently out of a six-year relationship, and not in the best mental space for serious dating yet – the idea of seeing a married woman casually really appealed to him.

I'm just after something low pressure with no expectations, he'd told me. *Plus, you seem cool and very easy to talk to.*

We have arranged to meet at a bar across the road from his apartment. It's been four weeks since Dane, and if all goes well and there's chemistry, I'll come back in another month from now for an overnight date with Ryan – or my 'bi-monthly hall pass' as I'd jokingly called it to my husband earlier.

I spot Ryan seated at a table by the window as soon as I walk in. He stands up when he sees me, his facing lighting up with a wide grin. He looks even better in person. He's taller and leaner than I expected, with wavy dark hair and a few days of stubble coating his angular cheeks and jawline. Not my usual type, but undeniably sexy in a dishevelled kind of way.

"Hey, you must be AJ, lovely to meet you!" Ryan says, leaning down to kiss me on the cheek. His refined British accent contrasts with his appearance and I warm to him immediately.

We order lunch and a drink each, and the conversation flows. It's light-hearted and fun, just like a first date should be.

There's definitely a mutual spark there in person. Ryan is very chatty and funny and smart and interesting. He's exactly the kind of guy I'd want to date, if I were single.

"Would you like another drink?" Ryan asks, watching as I finish off my second gin and tonic.

"Oh, I better not," I say, shaking my head, "I have to drive home after this."

"Hmm," Ryan says, looking at me thoughtfully. "How long do you have? I'm just across the road so we could go back and have a coffee and chat some more?"

I hesitate before responding. I'd told my husband I'd be home by 5pm – it's 2.15pm now. I'd also promised him that this was just a meet-up and nothing physical would happen; it seems a little risky going to Ryan's apartment.

"I guess I could come over for a quick coffee before I go," I say finally, grabbing my handbag from under the table.

"Nice bachelor pad here," I say, admiring Ryan's neat little apartment with its tea-coloured walls, dark-wood floors, and huge flatscreen TV.

"Ha, thanks." Ryan laughs as he fills a kettle in the kitchenette. "My ex and I had a couple of dogs, so she stayed at the house we rented with them, and I thought I'd move closer to work."

He hands me a cup of coffee and we settle on one of the black leather couches, sitting so close our knees touch. Even after over two hours together, the conversation hasn't dried up. It deepens now that we're in a private space.

"My ex was depressed for years," Ryan confides. "She was on antidepressants for so long, and I think they just made her emotionally blunted. One day, she told me she didn't want to be with me anymore. She was so cold about it."

"I'm sorry to hear that," I say. It resonates with my own experience on antidepressants. "I've been on them for a while now too, actually," I admit. "They do have that blunting effect. It's like I can still feel things but not as deeply as I used to – good or bad. I'm thinking I might stop taking them soon."

We talk for a while longer. I tell Ryan I'm not as happy as my Badoo profile states, and we compare notes on our relationships.

"It's really good to get all this out," he says, smiling warmly. There's a thirst in his eyes that mirrors my own.

When he pulls me toward him and kisses me, it feels unexpected yet completely organic. My lips melt into his, and my hands pull his body down onto mine. We kiss deeply, passionately, as my legs wrap around him.

Suddenly, in one swift move, Ryan picks me up off the couch and carries me through a door to his bedroom. I don't resist. *I shouldn't be doing this*, says a voice in my head as he pulls off my top and unhooks my bra. But I feel powerless in that moment and Ryan just feels so, so good…

"You're so beautiful," he says, his eyes taking in my naked body once he's finished undressing me.

I thank him and, sliding my hand into his jeans, place my hand around his cock and stroke it firmly; to my relief, it's long and rock-hard. He hurriedly puts on a condom he's grabbed from his nightstand, and turns me so I'm positioned on all fours. I moan with pleasure as he fucks me hard and deep.

After we've both reached a climax, I lie down on top of him, my head on his chest; and he hugs me tightly around my shoulders.

"I love that you're very cuddly as well," he tells me.

We roll over and he spoons me for a few minutes until I tell him I should probably get home to my family. I feel like I could happily stay in Ryan's arms for hours longer though.

"Today was fun," Ryan says once I'm dressed again and about to leave. "Hopefully you'll come back again when you can."

"Definitely!" I tell him, kissing him goodbye. It's hard to reconcile my guilt about sleeping with Ryan already with the euphoria I'm feeling after this afternoon with him. I decide I won't tell my husband though – I didn't intend for things to get so carried away after all, but if he knew, it could ruin everything.

On the drive home, I reflect on the afternoon with Ryan. *The sex was so good*, I reminisce, and also how *nice* it was to have that kind of stimulating conversation, that *connection* with someone again. Maybe that's what I've been missing.

> *Love is my drug*
> *like an addict's cocaine.*
> *Your touch on my skin*
> *sends warmth through my veins.*
> *Ecstasy and euphoria, come get me;*
> *leave the emptiness behind –*
> *let me pretend for a moment*
> *that instead of fucking my body,*
> *you're making love to my mind.*

CHAPTER 17

The Wave of Elation

We're supposed to be on a nice family walk together, but my husband seems glued to his phone screen.

"Who are you texting?" I ask, glaring at his phone in his hand.

"Just Sarah," he says, his voice defensive. "She's going through a hard time at the moment."

"Well, I'm sure she can wait. Can you put your phone away for a bit?" I demand, not bothering to conceal my irritation.

Sighing, he slips his phone into the back pocket of his shorts. "AJ, you've been texting people for weeks and weeks now – I talk to one woman and you get all pissy about it?"

"But we're on a family walk!" I protest. "We agreed we would keep anything with other people separate from family stuff."

"Fine," he says with a shrug, his tone flat.

We continue down the paved trail in silence, watching our daughter scoot ahead. The only sound is the scrape of the wheels on the concrete. I steal a glance at my husband, his arms swinging stiffly at his sides. Once upon a time we'd be holding hands, or his arm would've been lazily slung around my shoulder as we walked along, engrossed in conversation and laughter. I think wistfully of those moments, trying to pinpoint when they stopped. Did we not notice we'd stopped reaching out?

I briefly consider apologising for my hypocrisy – I do send the occasional text during 'family time', after all. But the words stick in my throat; it feels too late to fix the widening gap between us.

***

I'm sitting on the couch aimlessly scrolling through my phone that night when a WhatsApp message notification pops up. It's from Ryan. Finally. It will be a whole week tomorrow since we met and apart from a brief exchange after I got home again – acknowledging how nice the date was – I haven't heard from him at all. I'd sent him a quick message on Wednesday night, but every time I'd checked (far more often than I'm proud of), the WhatsApp ticks were stubbornly grey. I eagerly open Ryan's message.

Hey! It's been a busy week. Hope you've had a good one.

My heart sinks a little. The message feels dry, almost perfunctory, a far cry from the warmth and excitement in his earlier texts. Still, I try to match his tone, not wanting to seem needy or too keen.

Yeah, mine's been good. Are you up to much for the weekend?
there's a s
I'm riding high on this wave of elation,

on top of the world, feeling my best.
Blissfully ignorant of the crash to come,
as soon as I've reached the crest.
Before I know it, I'm coming down –
a rapid drop as the wave disappears.
I remember where I'm headed again:
to those familiar shores of despair.
I feel the flatness sink in now,
as I wash up on sands of resignation.
The wave has ebbed completely;
leaving just a memory
of its elevation.

I let myself sink deeper into the throes of self-pity for several more minutes until I hear the door creak as my husband comes in.

"What are you doing?" he asks, noticing me slumped on the couch with my phone in my lap.

"Nothing," I say, my voice sullen. "Just kind of upset with how this open marriage thing is going so far, I guess."

"Oh?" he asks, sitting down beside me. "Why is that?"

I tell him about how it seems to be fizzling out with Ryan, only a week after meeting him.

"I thought we had a really nice connection so I got my hopes up a bit," I admit. "It just makes me wonder if any guy would lose interest quickly seeing all the restrictions we have."

My husband sighs, as if he knows where this is going. "That's what we agreed to, AJ. You'll just have to try and meet someone else."

"But I don't want to meet a different guy every month or two!" I complain. "I just want one person who will keep in touch properly between catch-ups. Even if Ryan does want to see me again, I won't be into it unless there's some kind of sustained connection and build up to it."

My husband shrugs. "I don't know, AJ. Are we watching anything tonight?" he asks, clearly done with the topic.

"Well, what about Sarah? Are you planning to meet her soon?" I press.

He nods, his face serious. "Yeah, we're talking about booking a hotel and meeting in a couple of weeks."

I sit up straighter on the couch, intrigued. It's a morbid sort of curiosity. Weirdly, I'm impressed too, that my husband's managed to capture a woman's interest to the extent she's willing to stay over in a hotel with him.

"So, you're going to do an overnight with her straight away?" I ask, interrogating him now. "Have you even spoken to each other outside of texting?"

My husband reveals that he and Sarah have had a few phone calls and video chats already, to my surprise.

"We get along really well; she's a nice person." His voice softens as he describes her, and there's a warm gleam in his eyes.

"You said she's going through a hard time?" I ask.

He tells me that Sarah's at a breaking point in her marriage – she doesn't know how long she can go on with it as it is.

"I guess she appreciates having someone to talk to about it all," he adds. Something doesn't feel right to me though.

"Do you think she might be relying on you a bit much

for emotional support?" I ask him. "Or planning to try and use you as a jump-off to get out of her marriage?"

"No, AJ, Sarah's not like that!" my husband snaps, his tone defensive. He scowls at me, growing impatient. "Why all the damn questions?!"

"Sorry," I say, grabbing the remote and absent-mindedly flicking through the channels.

"Just one more question," I say a few minutes later, trying to sound light and breezy. "Has she sent you any nudes?"

"*What?!*" he sputters, taken aback. "No, of course not. It's not that kind of connection. We haven't even met."

He stares at the TV in silence for a few moments before turning towards me.

"Do *you* send guys nudes?" he asks, narrowing his eyes in suspicion.

His question catches me off guard. I falter for a moment, trying to figure out how to respond.

"Sometimes," I confess. "It's just part of the excitement of it all, I guess."

I watch his face fall as he processes this. I guess it can't be easy finding out other guys have images of your wife's naked body stored on their phones.

"I crop my face out of them, obviously," I lie, hoping to soften the blow.

"Well," he says slowly, his face breaking into a smirk, "would be nice if you sent some to me as well."

CHAPTER 18

Shared Connection

It's our daughter's first week at primary school and I'm finding the new morning routine is an adjustment. I'd had four years' practice getting her to daycare, but school is a whole new ball game, with having to make sure she's there in her full uniform with her packed lunch and all the right items in her bag, before the 8.45am bell rings. Luckily, there's been no clinging or tears so far.

By Thursday morning, we seem to be on top of things, so I let her watch TV for ten minutes while I change from my dressing gown to my work clothes. As I'm about to put on my blouse, I realise that I still haven't got around to sending my husband any nudes of me. *I probably should*, I think, especially as he's arranged to meet Sarah in Auckland this weekend. He'd checked with me on Monday night that this weekend was okay. I was proud of myself for being 'chill', even encouraging of it: "Yeah of course, it's about time you met someone," I'd said, adding, "hope it goes well for you."

Since then, though, I haven't been able to shake off my worry that Sarah will be hotter than me. *You have nothing to be insecure about*, I'd told myself firmly, *you have a fricken bangin' body*. Still, I decided against asking my husband to show me a picture of her, just in case she is.

I let my blouse fall to the floor and grab my phone. Would a topless photo in the mirror be best, or a selfie? I'm not exactly feeling very sexual this morning, so it's hard to get in the zone for it. In the end, I go for a selfie showing me from the waist up to hide that I'm still in my black work pants. I study the photo afterwards; I look a bit serious and it's not the most flattering angle of my smallish breasts, but it will do. I send it to my husband on Facebook Messenger and finish getting dressed.

***

I'm about to go on my morning tea break when my phone vibrates on my desk. It's my husband. I open his message.

Yummy! it says, with a wink and three heart emojis.

I cringe inwardly – a guy calling me *yummy* has always given me 'the ick'. I guess I'd rather not be described by a grown man in the same manner a child might squeal over a bowl of ice cream.

Glad you like x, I reply.

***

At dinner that night, we focus our attention on our daughter, who is telling us all about how her first week at school has been going.

"I've made four new friends already!" she says, beaming. "And we are allowed to get books from the library to take home!"

"You've been a very brave girl, I'm so, so proud of you!" I say, reaching over to give her a quick squeeze.

My husband is smiling at her dotingly from across the table. *He's such a proud dad*, I think.

"She's done amazingly this week, no issues at all," I tell him.

Our eyes lock for a moment, and I feel my heart swell a little with the knowledge that all the love and pride I have for our daughter is shared by him identically.

***

"Thanks for the photo today," my husband says, sliding into bed next to me later that night. "Made me a bit excited," he adds coyly as he draws me closer to him and begins to trace circles over my hip.

I feel my body stiffen against him and I pull away.

"I've been thinking," I say.

"Well, that's never good," he says, his voice playful.

I roll my eyes at him and continue. "I feel like maybe part of the reason I don't want sex much anymore is because for years now I've been forcing myself to just do it even when I haven't wanted to."

My husband frowns. "Why would you do that?" he asks, sounding confused.

"I don't know," I say. "I guess I worried that we'd end up having a sexless marriage if I didn't. But it's made it feel like a chore. I'm wondering if we should just not have sex unless we both really want to from now on?"

I'd been mulling over this for a few days now, since we had sex on Sunday night. I'd still had no further communication with Ryan and hadn't found anyone else to talk to yet either. So, in the absence of any fantasies of other men to enhance the experience, I was forced to be in the present. As usual, it was lacklustre, routine, passionless and dull. *Why am I even doing this if I don't enjoy it?* I'd asked myself, watching my husband's face contort as he pounded away at me in missionary.

My husband nods thoughtfully. "Well yeah, that makes sense," he agrees, with a touch of disappointment.

"What about tonight?" he asks after a long pause, his voice hopeful.

I sigh. "I don't think I'm feeling it tonight, sorry," I say. I feel guilty about turning down his advances, but I have to stick with my word – I can't just keep having sex with him out of obligation.

"Okay," he says nonchalantly, rolling onto his back.

I switch off the lamp on my nightstand.

"I've stopped my Sertraline this week," I inform him after a few minutes lying in silence. I hadn't planned to tell him tonight. But for the first time in a long time, the mood feels settled, peaceful between us – it seems like the right moment.

He turns to face me, his mouth opening in surprise.

"What, AJ?!" he asks, running his hand through his hair. "Why would you stop them? You know they help you."

His reaction is what I anticipated. I'm sure he remembers the worst of my pre-antidepressant days even more vividly than I do. I explain to him how I think the medicine has been making me feel emotionally blunted and I want to see how I feel without it.

"Plus," I add, "we seem to be in a more stable place now. I think, as long as I make sure I get enough sleep, I'll be fine."

He sighs loudly in exasperation. I can almost hear his eyes roll in the darkness.

"Well, make sure you go back on them if you start to feel anxious and depressed again," he says.

I reflect on the week with our daughter before saying goodnight.

"I can't believe she's actually five and at school already," I say, smiling.

"Yup, she's growing up crazy fast…" my husband says sleepily.

Even with the issues between us, I couldn't imagine not having someone to share these milestones and moments with. But is it a good enough reason to just try and suck up the fact that I don't feel the same way about him anymore?

It might be discovering
that she's learnt something new.
Or capturing a moment
that will be become a special memory.
Or maybe it'll be something she says
that makes us both laugh
as we all sit down for dinner.
I already know before I look up,
that when I meet your gaze

Shared Connection

*the surge of pride in your eyes
will mirror mine.
And your warm, joyful smile
will echo the love in my heart
that only you could possibly know.
It's in those moments it hits me
that even with how detached we've become,
I still feel it – that shared connection.
And she's worth fighting for.*

CHAPTER 19

My Blood Flows

The next day, I feel euphoric when I wake up. I have a heightened level of energy, as though I'm really excited about something but don't know what. It occurs to me I've been off Sertraline for a few days now – maybe it's just my brain chemistry adjusting. I'm not a neuroscientist, but it seems plausible.

I feel something else I haven't felt in a while too: horny. My husband's already left for work and my daughter's still asleep, so I stay in bed a bit longer and slide my hand down into my underwear. Closing my eyes, I surrender to the ecstasy of my slippery fingers. When I reach orgasm a few minutes later, I moan softly as my clitoris releases ripples of pleasure.

Mmm, I sigh, my heart pounding – orgasms are definitely stronger off Sertraline.

I feel antsy all morning at work, like I can't sit still. There are still remnants of a restless longing stirring within me – I need to meet someone new, I decide.

During my lunch break, I decide to download Tinder. Badoo is awful, I've conceded after swiping left through dozens of profiles all week. I'd never even heard of Badoo until it was suggested in my app store anyway – probably only guys who are desperate and can't meet anyone on the more well-known apps go on there. *There will for sure be much better guys on Tinder*, I think to myself optimistically.

The app requires me to allow location permissions on my phone so I can't manually set my location to Auckland – unless I pay an extortionate amount of money for premium membership, it seems. I feel a bit more blasé about anyone where I live spotting me on there now though – if they do happen to, well, they can just mind their own business. I create my profile, using the same bio and photos I did on Badoo, and set my distance preferences as far as Auckland. Unfortunately, I need to get back to my office before I have a chance to start swiping.

***

By the time I get home from work, my focus has shifted to my husband and his impending weekend in Auckland with Sarah. I'm getting out dinner ingredients when he comes in and dumps his work bag on the floor by the kitchen bench.

"What's wrong?" I ask him, noticing his glum expression.

"It's Sarah," he says sulkily, not looking up as he unties his shoes. "She can't meet this weekend anymore now – her and the kids are really sick."

The news takes me by surprise. I don't blame him for being in a bad mood – I'd be upset too if someone cancelled the day before we were supposed to meet.

"Sorry to hear," I say sympathetically.

He tells me that he called the hotel and has managed to move their reservation until the following weekend.

"Well, that's not so bad then," I say, grabbing my pre-workout banana from the fruit bowl. I feel a bit disappointed about his weekend with Sarah being postponed too, if I'm being honest. I'd kind of built myself up to it; mentally preparing myself for any uncomfortable feelings that might pop up while I know he's sleeping over with another woman. I'm not sure what feelings exactly – apart from my niggling worries over Sarah's potential 'hotness', I'd been feeling quite numb about the prospect of it all so far. But surely, I'll feel some kind of unease once I'm lying in bed wondering what they're doing together. Now I have to delay dealing with that for a whole week.

I feel sorry for him as well – not so much because he's let down about Sarah, but because it must be a bit demoralising to him that our respective extramarital date scores so far are 2–0. I try to shrug the guilt away; it's not my fault he hasn't been proactive enough, after all. But maybe, it's more a reflection of the fact that he only agreed to this in the first place to appease me. Maybe he's not cut out for an open marriage. *If that's the case though*, I wonder, *then how long can this go on for?*

***

Once my daughter is in bed that night, I settle on the couch and check through my phone notifications. Interestingly, there's a Facebook message from someone I don't know: Ben

Hudson. His profile is set to private but his profile picture shows a guy with wavy blond hair, blue eyes and a wide smile flashing a set of straight, white teeth. He's wearing a blue puffer jacket and there are snow-covered mountains in the background.

Damn, he's cute, I think, as I begin to read his message:

Hey, AJ. I promise you I don't normally do this, but I saw you on Tinder this afternoon and just found you so stunning and there was something about you that drew me in. I was worried you wouldn't see me on Tinder, so I decided to find you on here instead, I hope that's okay but totally understand if not.

I'm admittedly flattered at Ben's efforts to contact me – it was a bold move, bordering on intrusive, but it hints at a certain kind of determination that intrigues me. It does make me a bit nervous though – he must've only needed my first name and location to find me on Facebook so easily. I make a mental note to review my privacy settings later.

I decide to keep my response light and playful, with just a touch of flirtation:

Hey, Ben. Haha, well I wouldn't normally talk to Tinder people who stalk me on Facebook like this, but you're cute so I'll make an exception ;)

Ben is online and replies instantly.

Sorry! Your face is just so sexually attractive though… and the ethical non-monogamy thing; you seem so interesting and adventurous – I felt like I had to talk to you.

Ben's compliment about my face gives me a different buzz than being called pretty/stunning/beautiful, etc. It feels original and sexually forward without veering into crass and alludes to him having the kind of energy I want in a man.

We continue to chat and find out the basics about one another. Ben is thirty-three, lives in Auckland, and is a lawyer.

Of course, that explains why you know all the right things to say, I tease him.

He sends a laughing emoji and then tells me he has a girlfriend, but they are pretty casual and not exclusive yet.

So, we're kind of in a similar situation, he says.

He asks me what I'm looking for.

I'm looking for someone to see occasionally who excites me. I want dates and a real connection, not just sex – but my availability is pretty limited, I explain.

I brace myself for him to lose interest as I outline the rules of my open marriage. Ryan ghosted me, after all. But to my surprise, Ben replies almost immediately:

That all sounds perfect to me.

I reread his message, almost as if it's too good to be true. I begin typing a response, but he beats me to it.

I want to meet you – I'm actually going to be over your way loaning some ski gear to a mate in the morning. Would you have time for a drink in the afternoon?

My stomach flips, and I feel a rush of heat in my chest. *Oh my God*, I squeal internally like a fourteen-year-old girl, *he wants to see me tomorrow!*

I'll have to check with my husband, I reply.

Tomorrow should be fine :)

***

"My husband said I can only be an hour," I tell Ben as we sit face to face at a bar table with our wines. "I'm not really supposed to meet people in local places – we're quite private and he's worried about someone he knows seeing me."

My mind drifts back to the argument we'd had last night when I'd asked if I could meet Ben in a bar in town today.

"You're trying to bend the rules again!" he'd accused me. "We agreed – no local dates."

"No, we didn't," I'd countered. "We agreed that we couldn't meet anyone local – not that we couldn't meet anyone from another place locally."

He'd rolled his eyes. "Semantics, AJ."

I knew I was pushing boundaries again, but I needed to meet Ben and couldn't let the opportunity slip. He seemed worth the risk, and I'd told myself my husband would understand eventually.

In the end, we'd compromised: I could meet Ben for one hour, and if it went well, I could arrange an overnight date with him in two weeks. Obviously, it wouldn't have been two months since I'd met Ryan, but my husband never knew I'd slept with Ryan, and that didn't turn out as I'd hoped anyway. Therefore, it doesn't really 'count', I'd tried to justify it to myself.

Ben gives me a warm smile after I've told him about my silly time limit.

"I don't think you have anything to worry about here," he says with a laugh, gesturing around the mostly empty bar. "If anyone sees you though, just tell them you were getting legal advice."

My lingering guilt over upsetting my husband quickly dissolves and I feel my body relax in Ben's presence. It's only five minutes into the date, but it feels so calm and easy, as though we've known each other far longer than since yesterday.

He tells me about his job, how he's originally from the South Island, and his love of skiing. He asks me about my work, my daughter, and how the open marriage came about. I find myself opening up to him, loving how he doesn't take his deep-blue eyes off me. Occasionally, they flicker down my neck, over my tight, black, off-the-shoulder top, and towards my navel before returning to lock with mine. *I want him to kiss me*, I think dreamily.

Momentarily lost
in your ocean eyes
I think I'll stay here forever
however long that might be.

***

"Should I order another round or is this it for you?" Ben asks after I place my empty glass on the table.

"Oh shit!" I exclaim, my voice mildly panicked. "I completely forgot to keep track of the time." I switch on my phone screen: 3.57pm.

"We have three minutes left," I say, laughing with relief.

We leave the bar and Ben walks me down one of the busy main streets of town to where my car is parked.

"If you'd like, I'll book a hotel here the next time you're available; we can go out for dinner?" he says, looking at me intently. His voice is confident, but his face is hopeful, questioning, almost with a hint of worry that I'll say no – it's very endearing.

"Yeah, today was really fun. I'm definitely keen for that," I say, with a coy smile.

I reach up to hug Ben goodbye, and he kisses me on the lips. His lips are deliciously soft yet firm against mine, and as he pulls back, I can't resist – with my fingers laced through his sandy, blond hair, I draw his face towards mine and kiss him harder and deeper.

Reciprocating my intensity, his tongue locks with mine and a rush of electricity shoots through me. The press of Ben's erection against my jeans sends my blood flowing to my crotch… *Oh it's not fair*, I think, *I wish he could fuck me today…*

Suddenly, there's a series of loud car honks, startling us out of our public make-out session.

"Get a room!" shouts a male voice. I look towards the road and locate the source – a black Mazda slowly driving by with a car full of teenage boys jeering at us out the open windows.

"Oh, how embarrassing," I say, giggling as I cover my face with my hands.

Before reluctantly getting in my car, I tell Ben that I can't wait for our next date and say goodbye again – minus the PDA this time.

My blood flows through my veins,
like it always did.
Only today, I can feel it.
I will the days to speed up

until I see you again,
yet try to slow down the moments
that you're my future, not my past.
I savour the anticipation of you,
because the day will come,
and your touch will linger;
nothing but a memory on my skin.

CHAPTER 20

Self-Indulgence

I leave work thirty minutes early that Wednesday for an appointment at the sexual health clinic. I check in with the receptionist and take a seat while I wait. My visit here was spurred by a conversation with Ben during the weekend. To my relief, I'd received a message from him on Saturday as soon as he'd arrived back in Auckland:

It was great to meet you, AJ, I can't wait to see you again. I was so, so hard on the drive home after that kiss, throbbing the whole way.

The message ended with a grimacing-face emoji. It made me smile and also triggered a little throbbing in me as well.

Haha, that actually really turns me on, I'd replied. *If I had more than an hour, I would totally have got you to drive me somewhere private and fuck me right there in your car.*

Our messages after that became even more heated and explicit, leading to an avid sexting exchange that continued steadily throughout the entire weekend.

My loins were stirring with lust and my head was a million miles away as I went through the motions of parenting, running errands, and doing household chores. By Sunday night, I must've sent Ben the entire contents of the gallery in my phone's secure folder.

Your pussy looks incredible – I can't wait to be inside you, Ben had told me, clearly feeling the same way.

Then he made a suggestion that took me by surprise:

Hey, we should get STI tests before we meet next. That way we won't have to use condoms.

I'd replied to him that my husband was the only man I'd had unprotected sex with in years so he didn't need to worry about me having STIs.

We both should anyway, he'd said. *You can't be too careful these days.*

I appreciated his caution and how responsible he was being, so I agreed – I wanted to feel him inside me too, rather than a piece of rubber. I decided it was unnecessary to discuss it with my husband. I'd put that rule about wearing condoms on our open marriage contract as a precaution against STIs anyway – a test would be even safer, I'd reasoned.

"AJ?" says a voice suddenly, interjecting my thoughts.

I look up from my phone – a middle-aged woman with a short grey bob and kind eyes is standing in the waiting area, a bright smile on her face.

"Come this way," she says, and leads me down the corridor and into a small clinic with white walls and an examination table partially hidden by a dark-green curtain. She settles into a brown wooden chair, clipboard and pen in hand, and gestures for me to take the seat across from her.

The nurse introduces herself as Barbara and begins confirming my details.

"Now, I'm just going to ask a few other questions," she tells me, her voice warm but drawn out, as though speaking to a child.

"If anything makes you uncomfortable, love, then you aren't required to answer."

I take a deep breath, feeling a sense of unease – I've had cervical smears before but not specifically an STI test; I'm not sure what to expect.

Barbara asks if I'm sexually active and I say yes. Her next question puts me on the spot though: "Is it a new sexual partner, love?"

I shift in my seat, unsure how to respond. There's no way I want to tell her about our open marriage situation, she'd probably be horrified. But how could I explain why I suddenly want an STI check after being in a monogamous relationship for years?

I decide a simple white lie will be the best way to handle this. I quickly pull the left sleeve of my cardigan down, so it covers most of my fingers – hopefully Barbara didn't notice my wedding ring already.

"I've been seeing him for a couple of months now," I tell Barbara, with a shy smile. "We decided we want to start having sex without condoms."

"Aw that's great, honey, good for you," she says. Her praise is so genuine I almost feel proud of myself for being so sexually responsible.

She asks several more questions about my sexual activity then sends me behind the curtain. I remove my underwear, lie down on the table with a sheet placed over my legs and tell her I'm ready. I feel at ease again now as Barbara goes about extracting a sample from me. I'd prepared myself for having a swab shoved up my vagina – just not for invasive personal questions.

Once I'm done, Barbara hands me a slip to give reception.

"Thanks," I say, zipping up my boots.

"AJ?" she says, as I start to head out the door. I turn back to her.

"Is he really nice?" she asks sweetly, with a knowing smile.

I stare at her blankly, confused. "I'm sorry?"

"Your new man," she says, "is he really nice?"

"Oh yes," I gush, beaming at her. "He's just lovely." I can't help but feel pleased with my imposter skills as I leave the clinic.

Once outside, I revert to AJ – the married woman plotting a hotel sleepover with a guy she's only spent one hour with – and I drive home.

***

When I arrive home that afternoon after collecting our daughter from her after-school club, I'm surprised to see my husband's car parked in the driveway. He never mentioned finishing early. Inside, he's slumped over the kitchen counter, making a cup of tea.

"Daddy!" our daughter exclaims, running up to him with her arms open.

"Hello!" he says, scooping her up and kissing her head. His brightness feels forced, though – something is definitely off.

"You finished early today?" I enquire. He sets our daughter down and she darts off to the bathroom.

"Yeah, I asked if I could take the afternoon off; I was feeling average," he says, his tone flatter now.

"Are you sick? Is everything okay?" I ask, concerned. He exhales loudly, shaking his head.

"It… it's Sarah," he says, his voice breaking. "She called during lunch; she's called everything off."

"What do you mean, 'called it off'?" I ask, setting my handbag down on the bench. "You were supposed to meet her this weekend!"

He shrugs, folding his arms tightly across his chest.

"Yeah, well she told me her best friend confessed last night that he's in love with her and has been for years. She realised she feels the same way and has decided to leave her husband for him."

I stare at him and shake my head in disbelief. *What a soap opera*, I think scornfully.

"That really sucks for you," I say and offer him a hug. He stands stiffly, his arms hanging limply at his sides.

"I did say she might be looking for a jump-off," I remind him, a hint of smugness in my tone. A woman's intuition is always right though.

My husband looks at me with glum eyes.

"Maybe," he admits. "I'm pretty pissed, though – I spent $500 on a really nice hotel, and it's non-refundable."

"I'm hungry, Mummy!" our daughter announces, bursting into the kitchen. I sigh and grab her a yogurt and a few Ritz crackers.

"You want to watch *Peppa Pig* for a bit?" I ask. She nods eagerly, and I settle her on the couch in front of the TV.

I think for a moment then have an idea.

"Why don't you and I stay in the hotel?" I suggest to my husband as I return to the kitchen. The open-plan layout makes me lower my voice to avoid discussing Sarah within earshot of our daughter.

"What do you mean?" he asks, looking up from his tea.

"Well, I could see if Mum would babysit, and we could go up to Auckland for the night. Maybe it would be good for us."

The idea of a weekend getaway with my husband doesn't particularly inspire me, but it seems a shame to let a $500 hotel room go to waste.

He seems to think the same.

"Yeah, we could do, as long as your mum doesn't mind driving all the way here," he agrees, nodding slowly. "Makes sense to use the reservation."

"Sorry you have to replace Sarah with your wife," I say, smiling teasingly. I'm only half-joking though. I realise that by seeing Ben again the weekend after this one, I'll have been with three guys already – while my husband hasn't even had one date yet. At least him meeting Sarah would've evened things up a bit.

Later, I ask if he's still okay with me going ahead with my hotel plans with Ben.

"I just feel a bit bad about it," I say, "that you haven't met anyone yet."

"It's fine, AJ," he says. His voice is calm, but his face looks bleak. His sadness stirs guilt in me. Am I being selfish? Inconsiderate?

That's not your problem, I reassure myself. *The connection you can have with Ben might be exactly what you need to finally feel content.*

Self-Indulgence

It's a little self-indulgent, isn't it,
to allow myself to authentically feel,
to cast away the excuses I've made,
to stop denying my truths are real.

It's a little self-indulgent, isn't it,
to reject the road that lay ahead,
to not take the direction I'd planned,
to carve out my desired path instead.

It's a little self-indulgent, isn't it,
to put the spotlight back on me,
to no longer compromise or sacrifice,
to decide to do what makes me happy.

CHAPTER 21

Make Me Want to Stay

My post-Sertraline buzz seems to have completely worn off by Saturday morning. I'd noticed a steady dip in my mood over the last couple of days, as if a dark fog had descended upon me. My body felt stiff and heavy, which made everything seem like extra effort. My thoughts have seemed sluggish too, as if they kept getting stuck in places I didn't want to go.

The optimism and excitement from my earlier high had evaporated, leaving behind an aching void. Ben had been working late every night on an important case, so I didn't even have his messages to distract me.

I'd been plagued by the most intense dreams as well. In one, I watched as my body plunged off the edge of the cliff like the people in that disturbing horror movie *Midsommar*. I'd woken up in a cold sweat after seeing my face crushed into my skull on the ground below.

Another one I recall wasn't so nightmarish – it had involved my husband and I on the bedroom floor in a hot, steamy, lust-filled entanglement. He'd told me how beautiful I am and how much he loves me. Only, although the man in my dream looked like my husband, I had an awareness that it wasn't really him.

After hours of tossing and turning after waking abruptly at 3am, I check the clock again: 7.15am. *No point trying to get back to sleep now*, I think with a worried sigh.

Panicky thoughts race through my head. We're all set to go to Auckland later, but I've barely even slept; I don't feel like going now at all. We've organised with my mum for her to come around right after lunch so we can head away early. But I can't even remember the last time we both left our daughter for the night – what if she's upset and won't go to bed? Or worse yet, what if something happens to us, if we have a car accident, for example? *Snap out of it*, I try to reassure myself, *everything will be fine*.

Pulling myself out of bed, I wrap myself in my dressing gown and quietly head down the hall to the bathroom, careful not to wake my sleeping husband. My reflection in the mirror sinks my mood even lower. After a night of sleeping terribly, there are dark-purple rings under my eyes, and my skin is blotchy and lacklustre. *I look like crap*, I think, splashing cold water onto my face.

***

The room at the four-star hotel in Auckland my husband booked for his night with Sarah oozes simple luxury, with its plush burgundy carpet and crisp white walls.

"This is really nice," I remark, sliding open the doors to the private balcony overlooking the harbour. There's barely a cloud in the sunny blue sky and the breeze is mild, even though it's June now.

It occurs to me then, that, in all our years together, my husband has never thought to whisk me off for a romantic weekend somewhere like this. I feel a tinge of sadness hit me as I ponder what I've been missing.

I decide to check out the bathroom where there is a separate shower and a large, tiled bathtub. *Would they have taken a bath together?* I wonder. I picture their naked bodies entwined in the tub, talking softly together between kisses, in pure bliss just to finally be together in the flesh. The thought makes my stomach turn – not just from jealousy, but the irony that he'd once had that kind of intimacy with me.

My husband is reclined on the king bed against several pillows, playing on his phone.

"What should we do first?" I ask as I start to unpack my toiletries. He glances up and shrugs.

"Come here," he says, beckoning me to join him. I sit down beside him and he drapes his arm around my shoulder. Is this where we should rip each other's clothes off and have hot, passionate sex for an hour, finally able to reconnect as lovers in the absence of our child?

He looks at me and grins, forcefully, awkwardly. With his free hand he strokes my thigh, drawing little circles with his fingers, which, as usual now, make my skin crawl.

I remember as a child in the backseat of the car, my father would reach over and place his hand on my mother's leg in the passenger seat. "Stop that!" she'd chastise him, slapping his hand away almost instantly. I grew up confused about why she even married a man she felt so disdainfully about that she couldn't stand him touching her. Maybe she meant it when she said she hadn't always felt that way. Maybe the disconnection sneaks up on you so slowly that you don't notice until you find yourself swatting their hand away like a bug.

After only a few seconds, my leg begins to twitch and moves away from my husband, almost like a reflex.

I shrug my shoulders, breaking free of his hold. "Let's go for a drink," I say, standing up again. The hotel suite initially felt airy and spacious, but it suddenly feels claustrophobic.

***

After a drink at a nice rooftop bar down the road, we head back to the hotel to freshen up for dinner. I cover my under-eye circles with another layer of concealer and apply a coat of shiny pink lip gloss. *I look moderately presentable again*, I think, eyeing my reflection in the bathroom mirror.

I've booked a table at an Italian restaurant by the waterfront. I decided to wear a long-sleeved black bodycon maxi dress tonight, and I can't help but notice the admiring glances of the men we pass on the walk there. Well-dressed, well-groomed city-type men. *The type of men I go crazy for*, I think wistfully as I catch their eyes.

"You still get a lot of looks," my husband remarks with a bemused smile as we enter the restaurant.

"Oh really?" I ask innocently. "I hadn't noticed."

I feel more energised, animated amongst the ambience of the restaurant, with its rustic yet elegant charm, dim lighting, and muffled chatter of surrounding fellow diners.

"The reviews of this place were pretty accurate," I say, as I finish the last of my gnocchi dish. "It's really good."

"Indeed – good choice, AJ," my husband agrees, taking a bite of pizza.

Our dinner together has been pleasant so far, with the conversation – led by me, as usual – jumping from discussing our daughter, to gossip about friends and family members to potential holiday ideas.

"We could do a week in Queenstown," I suggest. "I really enjoyed my trip there last year."

The waiter comes over to take our empty plates and hands us each a dessert menu. In lieu of dessert, I opt to order another glass of rosé. It will be my third drink this evening. Annoyingly, the alcohol is starting to make me feel a bit agitated rather than merrily tipsy. *Maybe I'll feel better after this one*, I think, savouring the slight burn of the wine as it pours down my throat.

***

After settling the bill, we wander down to a quiet cocktail bar. I walk across the dark wooden floors to a sofa in the corner by a fireplace, trying to keep my margarita steady in my hand.

My husband sits beside me with his whisky sour. It seems we covered most topics during dinner; I can't think of anything to say now.

"It wouldn't hurt if you came up with something to talk about once in a while," I tell my husband, taking a sip of my drink. It was meant to be a gentle hint for him to initiate conversation more, but my tone comes out much more critical and accusatory than I intended.

He shoots an indignant look at me, hurt in his eyes. "AJ, you know I'm not a talker like you are. Plus, I thought we had really nice chats tonight."

I'm not satisfied by his response though.

"I wish you would understand how it is for me," I say, my voice rising with emotion. "I'm always the one making more effort – if I didn't say anything, I feel like you would just sit there saying nothing. It isn't about whether you're a talker or not, it's about bringing stimulation and energy, reciprocating."

My husband stares at me while I go off on my diatribe. After a few moments, he nods.

"I'm sorry, AJ, I'll try," he says finally, lowering his eyes to the glass in his hands.

We are silent for a few moments. I'd originally planned to avoid discussing the open marriage stuff tonight, but it feels like it's the only thing left to talk about now.

"Have you met anyone new on the apps since Wednesday?" I ask him.

I'd felt quite sorry for him after Sarah pulled out, so on Wednesday night I'd told him that to make it easier for him, he could have permission to meet girls who live in the same area as us. I figured if he and Sarah had lived closer to each other, they would've met a long time ago and we wouldn't have ended up with it all as imbalanced as it is now.

"The rule of not being allowed to meet anyone local would still apply to me though," I'd added.

My husband didn't seem overly enthusiastic about this special perk granted to him, but he agreed to try it.

He puts his empty glass down on the small mahogany table.

"I've been talking to one girl, Jess," he reveals. "She's keen for something casual with me."

"Well, that's good," I say, with a bright smile.

My husband's expression doesn't mirror my positivity though.

"I don't think Tinder is as easy for guys though, AJ," he says, turning back towards me. "I barely get any likes or matches. And when I do, most haven't read my bio properly and aren't interested once they find out I'm married. One woman basically abused me because she wouldn't believe that you knew I was on there."

His revelation surprises me. While I've had the odd judgemental comment, there's been no shortage of likes and matches – even with me being married and so far away from a lot of the guys swiping right on me.

"Oh," I say. "I didn't realise how hard it was." I twist the stem of my margarita glass in my fingers as I reflect on what he's told me.

"Do you think having an open marriage is working for us?" I ask.

He thinks for a moment then nods. "I think so," he replies. "Do you?"

I'm not sure how to respond. On some level, it is working – I have the freedom to experience the novelty of talking to someone new, hot sex with someone I've not been with for years, the chance to feel like a freer, sexier, more vibrant version of myself.

But at the same time, I can't deny that the guilt I have

for immersing myself in it more than my husband is starting to eat away at me. And deep down, while being with my husband already felt stale and stagnant, it was somehow more tolerable when I didn't know any different. Now it's like trying to adjust to the mundanity and dullness of everyday life after coming home from an exciting holiday to some exotic faraway place.

"I just think…" I begin, my voice trailing off. It's so hard to articulate it in words. "I just don't know if it's helping us," I say. "Everything still feels too platonic with us; I don't see how that can ever change. And it just doesn't feel like we're right for each other anymore. But having an open marriage doesn't seem like it will be sustainable long-term either."

My husband's eyes widen as I speak.

"What, so you want to stop the open marriage?" he asks.

I shake my head. *No, that's not what I want*, I think. *I don't even know what I want though.*

"No," I say, watching as a group of people leave the bar. "I don't know what I want."

My husband sighs and shifts his body away from me.

"Well, you need to figure out what you want, AJ."

With the mood having shifted from lukewarm to completely dead, we decide to head back to the hotel.

After finishing up washing my face and brushing my teeth, I climb into bed with my husband and switch off the light.

I'm not sleepy though. The margarita hit hard, and instead of making me feel better as I'd hoped, my earlier feelings of agitation are now surging through me in angry waves.

"What if we did a trial separation?" I blurt out in the darkness. The question came out of nowhere, taking the both of us by surprise. But maybe it's been lurking under the surface for a long time now.

"How would that even work, AJ?" my husband demands, sounding hurt and exasperated at the same time. "I can't afford to just move out somewhere. And my parents are too far away."

He's right, the idea is impractical. With a mortgage to pay and no family locally, there is no possible way either of us could just move out temporarily.

"We could have separate bedrooms for a while?" I suggest, knowing I'm clutching at straws.

"You said you would try, AJ," he says. "You've hardly tried at all."

I can't keep it together any longer. "How am I supposed to fucking try anymore?!" I cry. "There's nothing there!"

Now my eyes have adjusted to the dark, I can see the shadowy outline of his face. His black eyes bore into me and his mouth is fixed into a scowl.

"Well, did you even find a new therapist like you said you would?" he demands.

It reminds me, I never did get around to looking for a new one after that session with Rachel.

"No, I did not," I snap. "But why is everything always up to me? Why don't *you* find us a fucking therapist if you want to fix us so badly?!"

He continues to stare at me for a few more moments, probably wondering how the girl he married became this unhappy, raging woman.

"Goodnight, AJ," he says tersely, turning to face the other way.

At night in my dreams now,
it's often you that I see.
Except it's not really you,
just who I wished you would be.
Seeing me how I wanted,
loving me in the right way.
Saying the things I needed to hear
to make me want to stay.

CHAPTER 22

Undoing

The bump of the car pulling into our driveway stirs me awake. Nursing a hangover from the night before, I'd slept most of the way home from Auckland. My head is sore, but not pounding like it was when I woke up this morning, fortunately. I still feel like I might throw up at any minute though.

Since getting up this morning, my husband hasn't spoken to me other than when completely necessary, even as we got brunch together after checking out of the hotel.

Rubbing my sleepy eyes, I notice he's pushing the button on the small remote control for the garage door.

"What are you doing?" I ask groggily, as he drives into the garage. He normally parks alongside my car out on the driveway.

"The paint's peeling on the roof," he explains. "I'm gonna park in the garage from now on to stop it getting worse."

"What?!" I exclaim, feeling much more alert suddenly. "Can't you just get a cover for it or something? You can't park here; it's our gym area!"

We get out of the car and unload our suitcases from the boot.

"AJ," he counters, a note of defiance in his tone, "the car isn't covering the exercise mats; there is still plenty of space to work out in."

"Maybe for *your* workouts," I argue. "I use the whole garage for mine."

"Well too bad," he mutters, rolling his eyes.

We continue to bicker about it as we go into the house.

"Mummy! Daddy!" our daughter greets us happily. She's sitting at the breakfast bar with a wooden spoon and a mixing bowl.

"Hi, darling!" I say, giving her a hug.

"Me and Nana are making pikelets," she tells me.

"Did you have a nice time away?" my mum asks.

I glance at my husband. I'm not sure 'nice' would be an accurate description for our failed weekend rendezvous.

"Yeah, it was good," he tells her with a tight smile.

When he takes our suitcases off to the bedroom, Mum's smile disappears and she gives me a concerned look.

"What were you two arguing about before – is everything okay?" she asks, her voice hushed.

"He wants to keep his car in the garage now, he knows I need it for my workouts," I complain to her. "He's completely unreasonable sometimes," I add, hoping for some sympathy.

She sighs.

"Well, AJ, you aren't very easy to live with sometimes either, you know," she says, no doubt remembering her constant battles with me as a moody teenager.

***

We all eat the pikelets they've made, and then my mum takes our daughter out to the playground and shopping for the afternoon. I have a nap for an hour to catch up on yet another night of terrible sleep.

Afterwards, with my hangover mostly worn off, I decide to see how a workout will go with the reduced space. The area that's left, amongst my husband's car as well as the lawnmower, wheelbarrow and workbenches, is only about two square meters. Not nearly enough for all the exercise I do in my circuits. Plus, with the windows only able to marginally open, the garage reeks of car fumes. I consider opening the garage door, but I don't fancy everyone passing by to see me working out in my tiny shorts and sports bra.

Feeling frustrated, I storm back into the house, where my husband is gaming in the study.

"I need you to move the car," I interrupt him, giving him a sharp tap on the shoulder.

"For fuck's sake, AJ," he says angrily, standing up from the desk chair. "I told you; I'm not moving it – I cannot afford for the paint to get any worse right now."

"That's ridiculous!" I cry. "Every other car is fine outside!"

He refuses to budge on it though.

"You're so fucking stubborn!" I shout at him, silently thankful that our daughter isn't here to hear all of this.

My accusation appears to anger him even more. "AJ, you are the stubborn one; you can't just have everything your way all the fucking time!"

I observe my husband then, with an almost cold indifference. He looks so pathetically contemptuous with his jaw clenched and his fists shaking with fury at his sides. *This isn't even about the car*, I think.

"Look at you," I snap, my voice dripping with scorn. "You just need to go get fucking laid."

Oh no you did not say that, AJ, I groan to myself. But it's too late, I can't take back my last words.

My husband glares at me, stunned by my harsh remark.

"Fuck you, AJ, just fuck off."

"Fine," I say. At that moment, I hear the muffled voices of my mum and daughter as they come in the front door.

"AJ," he says, as I start to head out to see them. I look back at him.

He looks at me directly in the eyes, his face darkening.

"If I wanted to get laid, Jess would have me at her house ASAP."

***

My anxiety seems to have a 3am alarm clock. *Not again*, I think, *I've been waking up at this time for no reason for over a week now.*

I glance at the empty space beside me in the darkness. My husband and I had managed to keep up appearances yesterday until my mum headed home after dinner. He'd disappeared off to his study after our daughter went to bed, as usual, but he hadn't come to join me in the lounge later.

I had been struggling to stay awake enough to focus on anything, so by 9.30ish, I decided to call it a night. To my surprise, out in the hallway, all the lights were off and the door to the spare bedroom was closed. It took a second for it to dawn on me what it meant. My husband had never slept in the spare room before. Our fight must've pushed him over the edge, I realised. Was it really that bad though?

I'd fallen asleep quickly after getting into bed, physically and emotionally spent. But now I'm wide awake, ruminating on our deteriorating relationship.I think back to past times when, after a fight, I'd beg for forgiveness if I'd upset him. I hated going to bed mad, so I'd insist we talk it out until we came to a resolution. Sometimes we'd have make-up sex.

But now? I picture him asleep in the spare room next door, a wall between us, and me, here alone, not missing him at all.

> *I've spent hours undoing us,*
> *trying to figure it out;*
> *when the glue came unstuck,*
> *where the seams came undone,*
> *how once-stable foundations*
> *became shaky.*
> *Once I peel back the layers though,*
> *I realise that the woman there –*
> *the one back where we started –*
> *I'm just not her anymore.*
> *Maybe that's our undoing.*

CHAPTER 23

Not Done After All

Three kilos less than a month ago. I step off the scale and study my naked reflection in the mirror. My tired eyes are dark and sunken, my cheekbones look sharp, and my collarbone juts out from my shoulders. *My anxiety really is eating away at me*, I think sadly, noting that even my breasts have shrunk.

My husband left for work while I was showering, not coming into the bathroom to say goodbye as he normally would.

After dropping my daughter at school on the way to work, I hear a strange but painfully familiar crunching sound while I'm backing out in the busy school car park. The last time I heard that sound was when I was about seventeen and had accidentally hit my dad's car in the driveway.

In a panic, I stop reversing and jump out of the car. Assessing the damage, I realise I've reversed into the left side of a black station wagon that's now stopped in the middle of the car park. To my dismay, it has a large dent, and so does my little Suzuki Swift.

I swear I checked for cars coming past, I think, angry at myself for my carelessness.

The driver, an elderly man, probably a grandparent of one of the students, gets out and approaches me.

"I… I'm so sorry! I should've seen you," I stammer, my face burning.

"It's alright, these things happen," he says calmly, with a kind smile.

After giving him my details, I return to my car and immediately burst into tears. Within moments, my shoulders are heaving against the steering wheel as I sob uncontrollably.

I grab my phone and manage to text my boss through blurry eyes: *Sorry, I'm not feeling well so won't be in today.*

When I get home, I immediately strip off my work clothes and put on my dressing gown before crawling into bed for another crying session.

At least an hour later I'm able to get myself together enough to sit down with my laptop.

After organising my car to be booked in at the panel beaters, I open a new tab and type *therapists near me* in the search bar.

With how much of a complete mess I've been lately, I've decided I need to talk to someone who is a proper therapist, not just a couples' counsellor.

There's one who catches my eye. She's a Chinese lady and her website says she's a psychotherapist and specialises in couples therapy and interpersonal relationships. *Perfect*, I think, dialling her number into my phone.

"Hello, this is Feng," says a sweet voice with an accent after a few rings.

I tell her my name and that I'd be interested in making an appointment for couples' therapy with my husband, and possibly individual therapy for myself as well.

"I don't have any free appointments until the first week of July," she says. I mentally calculate the dates – that's almost three weeks away.

"Oh okay," I say, "I'd hoped for something sooner but that will be fine."

Feng senses my disappointment. "Sorry, it's very, very busy at the moment. I will need to do an initial phone consultation with you before we meet – we could do that now if you have ten minutes?"

At least that's something, I think. She asks me to describe my situation. In my emotionally raw state, I find myself pouring my heart out to Feng about everything – my dissatisfaction with my husband, my depression and anxiety, my moods, even the open marriage and my desire for sex and connection with other men.

"You haven't been fulfilled!" Feng says emphatically after I've finished speaking. "You were trying to fill the emotional void that exists within your marriage. You've wanted to feel seen, to feel validated!"

The understanding and lack of judgement in her response surprises me. Apart from Rachel, I'd never spoken to any kind of therapist before – I hadn't expected her to speak to me as though she was reading me; it was oddly comforting.

"Yes!" I agree, already starting to feel better. "That's exactly it."

I disclose to Feng that my husband thinks most of the

issues with our marriage stem from my anxiety. "He even said I might have borderline personality disorder," I add.

He didn't directly say that as such; I'd sent him a link to an article I'd found down a Google rabbit hole last week while trying to figure out what's wrong with me.

"Do you think I could have this, maybe?" I'd asked. He admitted that, yes, I did seem to have a lot of the symptoms.

Feng tells me that even if I exhibit traits of borderline personality disorder, they would have to be very severe to meet the criteria for a diagnosis.

"And, from what you've told me, these traits are mostly only present in the context of your relationship," she says. It's both a relief that I probably don't have that, as well as a disappointment – it would've been helpful, having a label to account for my multitude of issues.

Feng suggests I start taking my Sertraline again if it was helping me feel more in control of my emotions.

"Discuss it with your GP, of course. But for some people, antidepressants are necessary," she says. "If you do want to taper off, it may be better to wait until you've had some therapy and feel in a better space."

I ask Feng if she thinks it's possible my marriage can be salvaged.

"It could be," she says thoughtfully. "It's about breaking negative relationship cycles and working out how you can re-establish your emotional connection. Remember, AJ, even if you were with someone else, you wouldn't have these exact problems you do with your husband, but in any relationship, there are problems; there is no perfect relationship."

"I guess so," I reply. Truthfully, I think I'd prefer any

problem over not being in love with or attracted to the man I'm supposed to be with for the rest of my life though.

After the call is over, I message my husband.

I'm sorry for what I said last night, I didn't mean it. I've booked an appointment for us to see a therapist at the start of July.

Five minutes later, he replies: *Thanks, AJ, hopefully it will help.*

Standing up from the couch, I take a deep breath and sigh, as if letting all the tension of the day out of my body. I know what I need to do now. I head to the kitchen and grab a red container off the top shelf of the pantry. I search through the stacks of medicine boxes inside, until I find it – a little pink box buried at the bottom, with *Sertraline* printed on the label.

> *Somehow thought I was stronger now*
> *Emotionally okay enough to manage without you*
> *Realised how wrong I was though, as here we are again…*
> *The familiar tightening of my chest*
> *Racing thoughts surging through my mind*
> *And the knot in the pit of my stomach*
> *Little white pill, looks like we're not done after all*
> *I swallow and surrender to your promised anaesthesia*
> *Not long until my body will be calmed, my thoughts pacified*
> *Eventually I'll try to live without you – just not yet.*

CHAPTER 24

Stuck

Hey, how are you? Did you have a nice weekend in Auckland? Only four more sleeps to Saturday now… can't wait x

I smile as I read Ben's message.

Hey, I'm good. Weekend didn't go amazingly, had fights with husband that kinda killed the mood a bit, haha.

Oh no! Ben replies. *I hope that you are okay now? And that it's still alright for you to see me this weekend?*

Ben's concern is sweet but it makes me think I shouldn't have let him know about my marital problems; I don't want him to worry about me.

Yeah, we are all good now, I say. *My husband might be meeting a girl one night next week anyway, so definitely fine for me to see you still!*

After he got home last night, I'd told my husband what Feng had said during the phone consultation, and also that I'd started my medication again. I'd broken down in tears again during the conversation, feeling overwhelmed by it all.

"You definitely do need your medication, AJ," my husband replied, looking at me sympathetically. He seemed relieved that he might have some reprieve from the neurotic, unstable version of me soon as well. We were cordial to each other during dinner and even watched a movie together later.

"Are you still okay with me doing the hotel thing this weekend?" I'd asked him once we were in bed.

"You might as well, AJ," he'd said, yawning. "I'm probably catching up with Jess next week."

"It's good you're not leaving that too long," I'd told him, giving him a hug goodnight.

***

I wake up on Saturday morning feeling a nervous kind of excitement – I can't believe the day has arrived. At least I'd managed to sleep for seven hours straight so I look well-rested and won't feel tired tonight. I guess the Sertraline effects are kicking in again.

That morning, my husband and I take our daughter to her ballet class, followed by a visit to Bunnings for some new tools he needs.

After lunch, I take a second shower, making sure I'm fully shaved and smooth in all the right places, and do my hair and make-up for the evening with Ben.

At 3.50pm, the time has finally rolled around to go meet Ben at the hotel he's booked.

At the end of our driveway, a man with a Border collie is waiting for me to pull out before he can resume walking. I slow the car to a halt and wave at him to signal that I'll wait for him. He hesitates and waves back, which I assume means he'll let me pass him first.

Then, both with our wires crossed, I pull out at the same time he carries on walking. I slam on my brakes as he yanks his dog back on the leash. He glares at me, his face flashing with shock and anger.

"You fucking stupid bitch!" he yells, as he passes the front of my car, shaking his fist at me.

"Sorry!" I mouth, tears springing to my eyes.

My near-miss of almost running over a man and his dog dampens my spirits on the ten-minute drive to the hotel, but the incident leaves my mind as soon as I see Ben waiting for me in the foyer.

He's as handsome as I remembered from our first date, standing there dressed in a red-and-black checkered shirt and dark-blue jeans, his face lit up with a warm smile.

Taking my suitcase, he guides me into the lift and presses the button for the third floor. Once we exit the doors into the empty corridor, he puts my suitcase down for a second to pick me up, and with my legs wrapped around his waist he carries both me and my suitcase to his room. It's the first time a man has ever literally thrown me down on the bed and I love it.

Ben lies on top of me and kisses me deeply, hungrily, while his hands take off my clothes and run over my breasts and down my legs, teasing me in between my thighs. I unbutton his shirt, revealing his taut, smooth body. Within moments we are both naked and his bare cock is thrusting deep inside me.

"That was so hot," Ben says about five minutes later as we lie naked and breathless in each other's arms. "Sorry I didn't last long; I was so excited driving here to see you again."

We both freshen up, and that evening walk a couple blocks to a little Japanese restaurant I'd chosen for dinner and drinks.

While Ben had made a great first impression on me, I'm even more smitten with him now after getting to know him better, and although the restaurant is full, I feel like Ben is the only person in the room.

He confides in me about the situation with his 'casual girlfriend'.

"She's wanting to keep things casual while she focuses on her studies. But I think after that we'll take the next step, become exclusive," he says, picking up a piece of sashimi with his chopsticks. "I'm not sure though, she's great, but I keep having niggly feelings that she's not the right person."

"I thought my husband was the exact right person for me once," I say wistfully. "But he's not. I don't even know if I believe there's a right person anymore."

Both a little intoxicated after several wines and cocktails, we decide to head back to the hotel, where we collapse on the bed again. It's all a delicious, blurry haze as we kiss and stroke each other's bodies. I enjoy how he pulls my hair back to gaze at my face while I go down on him.

A couple of hours later, we are both exhausted. Ben spoons me from behind for a bit and then rolls over and falls asleep. I have to fight the urge to cuddle up next to him so I can be in his arms all night.

As we stir awake the next morning, he pulls me in toward him and enters me from behind, his arms wrapped around me and hands caressing my breasts. Even though I'm tired and nauseous and my head is pounding, I'm in heaven at that moment.

After we're up, and showered and dressed, Ben checks out of the hotel and we drive in his car to a nearby café for brunch, then a short walk around the gardens. He puts his arm around me as we walk together and it occurs to me how risky it is; I mean, what if someone I know saw us? I don't really care to explain why I'm on a romantic stroll with another man.

"I should really get going back, I have lots of prep to do for a case starting tomorrow," Ben says. We drive back to the hotel, where my car is parked.

"Thanks for a really nice night," I tell him, as we hug and kiss goodbye.

"You too," he says. "Hopefully we can do it again soon."

As I drive home to my husband and daughter, I'm hit with an unsettling sense of nostalgia for the night with Ben, and the version of myself I left with him in the hotel car park.

***

My husband is unloading the dishwasher when I walk in the house. I remove my coat and shiver at the chill in the air.

"Why isn't the heat pump on?" I ask him, hanging my coat by the door. "It's freezing in here."

"I only just got home," my husband says, his voice defensive. He tells me our daughter was invited to a playdate for the afternoon.

"How was your night?" he asks, standing up straight and crossing his arms.

My night was amazing of course, but now, compounded by lack of sleep and a mild hangover, my mood is flat and depressed, and my mind is in utter turmoil.

I take a deep breath, knowing what I'm about to tell him won't go down well.

"I can't do it anymore," I say, lowering my eyes to the floor.

"What do you mean, you can't do it?" he asks, looking puzzled.

"The open marriage," I continue, "I can't do it. It's making everything too confusing for me."

My husband stares at me for a few moments, his face hardening.

"AJ, we agreed we'd keep doing it while we sort things out with us. I told Jess I'd meet her next week; you can't just pull the plug on everything just because it doesn't suit *you* anymore."

My husband's reaction surprises me. I'd expected him to be exasperated by me flip-flopping on things again, but not so adamant about persisting with the open marriage.

"I'm sorry," I say, my voice cracking with emotion. "I can't do the open marriage. But I can't go back to the way it was before either. I just feel so stuck. I need us to have separate rooms for a week while I figure things out."

"What, like a break?!" he asks incredulously, his eyes scanning my face as if to ascertain how serious I am.

I nod slowly, feeling tears roll down my cheeks.

"Yes, a break. For a week," I confirm. "There's no other way."

My husband doesn't try to argue with me anymore. "Fine," he says. "But you can be the one to sleep in the spare room."

It's fair, I guess.

Too often my emotions would guide me,
urging me to follow my heart.
How foolish I was though,
to fall for their egotistic games
and believe their selfish deceptions.
They always promised so much happiness
yet hid the price I'd pay for it.
Sometimes pleasure isn't worth the pain,
so, I tried to break free from the chain,
to trust my mind to lead the way.
And that's hiw I found myself here,
stuck in my indecision.

CHAPTER 25

Today Marks the Day

Today marks the day
I opened my eyes to a different room.
I wanted to yearn for your presence,
but I didn't feel like anything was missing.
Today marks the day
I heard you leave the house without saying goodbye.
I admit that it hurt a little,
but I was relieved not to have to say 'I love you'.
Today marks the day
I stepped outside, feeling terrified.
Too many unknowns, so much uncertainty,
but I couldn't ignore how curious I was.
Today marks the day
I felt as though life as I knew it ended.
I told myself to fight for it, to try and hold on,
but I think I like how it tastes;
this bittersweet freedom.

CHAPTER 26

The Limit

I keep getting flashbacks of our night, Ben's message says. *You felt so, so good. I'm so glad we got those STI tests so I could be inside you properly.*

To my relief, he's been pretty consistent with messaging me since our night together.

I wish we didn't have to wait so long until next time, he says, adding, *it will be worth it though.*

I sigh, adjusting a throw blanket around me on the couch. I should probably come clean.

In my message to Ben, I tell him my husband and I are having a break this week while I work out what I want.

Ben sees my message, but it's five minutes before he replies.

Oh shit, I'm really sorry to hear. I hope I haven't caused any problems??

No, it wasn't you, I assure him, *I just don't think that having an open marriage is sustainable for us.*

It's already Thursday night, but I'm really no closer to making a final decision than I was on Sunday.

I've made lists of reasons I should stay and reasons I should leave, but how do I weigh them? Is my desire for freedom, autonomy, and the chance to find a more fulfilling relationship more important than my daughter growing up in a stable, nuclear family where she sees both parents every day? Would it be better to wait until she's left home? Could I even afford to be a single mum?

According to a rough budget I put together, I'd barely have any disposable income on my own. *Definitely no fancy holidays to places like France in the future*, I think sadly.

But then, so far, I am admittedly enjoying my nights alone, chatting to people, writing poems, watching whatever show I want. I'm enjoying the silence of the bedroom at night, undisturbed by my husband's light snoring. And with so much distance between us, my guilt about not having sex with him has disappeared. None of my reasons for staying are actually about wanting to be with him, I realise.

We could keep going with the open marriage – for the sake of our daughter. But deep down, I know that if I meet someone like Ben, I won't want him for stolen weekends or to be a side piece. I'll want more. But what if someone like Ben never comes? What if I upend my daughter's life for nothing? I could end up completely alone.

But isn't alone better than this? I ask myself.

My husband has been giving me the silent treatment all week, which hasn't helped my decision-making process. We still sit down for family dinners, and he thanks me briskly for the meal, but the rest of the time, he speaks only to our daughter. When we pass each other in the hallway, he looks straight ahead, as if I'm not even there.

"I don't understand why you're being so hostile to me," I'd said to him earlier, while our daughter was in the bath.

He had raised his eyebrows and stared at me questioningly. "What did you expect, AJ?" he'd muttered under his breath.

> *Your once-gentle eyes*
> *hardened in a robotic stare.*
> *The coldness in your voice*
> *says we're broken beyond repair.*
> *Your ghost-like presence;*
> *a shadow of what used to be –*
> *it haunts me as a reminder*
> *of the death of you and me.*

***

The next night, I've finally reached a decision. I ask my husband to join me in the lounge for a discussion once our daughter is asleep. It's hasn't quite been a whole week since we started our 'break' but I think it would be nice to get it all out of the way before the weekend.

"So?" my husband asks, his tone flat as he takes a seat on the other couch.

I'm feeling calm and quietly optimistic about what I'm about to tell him.

"I've been going over things in my head all week," I begin. "I've also started to feel much better after starting the medication again – I can think more clearly."

He listens to me with a blank expression but doesn't say anything, so I keep going.

"I want us to give therapy a real go, and I'll also get my own therapy to work on my anxiety. And we could keep the open marriage going as it is now, and review in another six months."

He still doesn't speak. My stomach begins to tense.

"What are you thinking?" I ask.

He looks down at his hands clasped in his lap and shakes his head.

"AJ," he says finally, clearing his throat. "I've been reflecting on everything this week too. I don't want to keep dragging things out anymore. It's over."

The finality of his words shocks me.

"What?!" I ask. "What do you mean it's over? This break was so I could think about things."

He raises his head and looks into my eyes with disdain as he speaks.

"It's always been about you, AJ, always about what you want; your anxiety. What you have been doing to me over the last year, even the last few years, is emotional abuse. What you want changes all the time, I can't handle it anymore. You've broken me."

"This isn't about my anxiety!" I protest, my eyes stinging with tears. "But even if it is, I told you I'm going to get help… Why wouldn't you be more supportive?"

He sighs and shakes his head again.

"AJ, I've tried to support you. But I need to prioritise my own mental health. We are separating, and that's it."

He retreats to the study, leaving me sobbing on the

couch as I let his words sink in… We are separating… and I have no control over it anymore.

I sleep fitfully that night and have another dream about my husband; not a sex dream this time though. Instead, I'm chasing him through a crowded train station as he runs from me, calling and calling to him, but he won't turn around. *I've lost him forever*, I think. I wake with a surge of panic at 3am, a deep, gnawing ache in the pit of my stomach.

The following morning, I'm sitting at my laptop in the lounge while my daughter eats breakfast when he comes in and makes his coffee.

"Can you come read this poem?" I ask him. "It's called *The Limit*; I wrote it the other week."

His expression is sombre as he reads the words on my laptop screen.

"It was a self-fulfilling prophecy, AJ," he says once he finishes, his voice unwavering.

I took off my mask for you,
revealed my darkest thoughts and deepest pain.
I let you see all the crazy inside me
and you still didn't think I was insane.
I told you all the true reasons
for the lingering sadness in my eyes.
You didn't run away though,
just held me against you as I cried.
I projected on you my weaknesses,
pointed out all the things that were wrong.
But no matter how much I broke you,
I knew it would never make me strong.

The Limit

I didn't make it easy to love me at times,
but you kept on doing it anyway.
Everybody has a limit though –
and I knew I'd push you to yours one day.

CHAPTER 27

How I Knew

My husband decides he will go to his parents' a few hours further up north that weekend and break the news to them. I suggest he take our daughter for the trip.

"They'd love to see her," I say. "Besides, I don't know I can cope with her alone all weekend right now."

Thankfully, he agrees. After they head away shortly before noon, I ponder how I'll fill the hours while I have the house to myself.

After a long meditative walk along a nearby bush trail, I return home and call my mum.

"We've decided to separate," I say, not long after we've exchange greetings. There's silence at the other end.

"What?!" she asks finally, stunned. "I thought you were going to talk to someone?"

I tell her about the last week, and my husband's final decision. I'd previously told her, in confidence, that we were trying an open marriage, but she'd been appalled by the idea so I hadn't gone into much detail about it since.

"I told you it was a silly idea, seeing other people," she accuses after I've finished retelling the events of last night. "He's a good husband. You're going to ruin your life doing this."

"It wasn't my decision!" I cry angrily, shocked at her reaction. "I haven't been happy with him for years and years though, you know that!"

"I know, AJ," she says, her voice softer now. "It's just so sad is all, I'm really worried about you."

"I know. Can you let Dad and Holly know?" I ask, referring to my sister. "It's just easier than having to tell everyone individually."

After the call, I decide to do some online research to see what our next steps are.

Apparently, in New Zealand you can't file for divorce until you've been separated for two years. But we need to work out a separation agreement and figure out how we will split the assets. I realise that because my husband earns more, he will be the one who likely gets to keep the house, and I'll have to move out somewhere, either a really cheap house or a rental.

We'll have to work out a custody schedule for our daughter. And tell the rest of our family, and our friends and work colleagues… I feel like I've been putting on a happy face to everybody over the last few months, even while it's felt like my world has been crashing down around me. How will we possibly tell everyone; what if they react the same way my mum did?

I close the laptop, feeling overwhelmed. It's all just too much.

I draw myself a hot bath and reflect on what my mum said as I lie there.

Maybe she's right, maybe he would come around. If I pleaded with him, absolutely grovelled, promised that I'd work on myself. I'm sure he'd change his mind eventually.

I close my eyes and surrender to the warm comfort of the water, melting the tension away from my tired body.

Gradually, my mind starts to shift as I realise he's right, it needs to end. There's no point dragging on the fights, the disconnection, or the emotional roller coaster of the open marriage. Maybe therapy would help some of our issues, but it wouldn't magically reverse our incompatibilities so we could be happy together again. And, I admit to myself, this past week has allowed me to see that I feel more content alone now than when I'm with him.

Maybe that's how, ultimately, I know separating is the right decision.

After the bath, I pick up my wedding and engagement rings I left on the vanity. But instead of putting them on again, I store them away in the bottom of my jewellery box.

I didn't know how bad it had become
because of the heated exchanges
of hurtful words,
or the tears of frustration
from not being heard.
I didn't know had bad it had become
because of the endless talks
that went around in circles;
revealing more problems than answers.

How I Knew

It was the peace upon waking
to an empty space beside me.
It was the sense of autonomy,
in place of dependency.
It was the realisation
of how much more content I felt,
without you.
That's how I knew.

CHAPTER 28

The Unknown

"How did your parents take it?" I ask my husband when he returns on Sunday afternoon. He grabs a beer from the fridge and cracks it open.

"They were pretty upset," he says, "but they said if there's anything we need to let them know."

We never told his parents about the open marriage, which might explain their more sympathetic reaction than my own mother's.

My husband takes a swig from the can. "They also wanted me to pass on, AJ, that they'll always consider you part of the family."

I'm touched at the kindness of the relayed message from my in-laws; even though I was apparently the 'favourite' daughter-in-law, it's not what I was expecting at all.

"What are you talking about?" our daughter asks as she comes back from the bathroom.

"Should we tell her now?" I ask him. He nods, his eyes mirroring the feeling of dread growing inside me.

We sit our daughter between us on the three-seater and explain to her our decision to separate, in a way that hopefully makes sense to a five-year-old.

"You may have noticed Mummy and Daddy have been fighting lots lately," I say, putting my arm around her shoulder. "We've decided it's best for us all if I move to a different house; you'll get to have turns living with both of us."

My heart breaks watching as my daughter's face falls. She begins to cry.

"No!" she says defiantly. "We can't do that! Can't you just say sorry to each other?!"

If only it were that simple.

"It will be a big change," my husband tells her, biting his lip. "But remember that we love you very much still."

I guess we've said all the right things, I think. *It doesn't make it any easier though.*

***

That night, I tell my husband about my findings on the separation process.

"It will be pretty straightforward," he says. "We can just do our own separation agreement, no need for lawyers."

He tells me he will buy me out of the house. "Remember I put more money towards the house deposit, the mortgage, and spent more on doing up the house, so I'll work it out based on that."

I stare at him trying to make sense of what he's saying.

"You mean I'll end up with less than you? The law is a fifty-fifty split though!"

He sighs. "That's completely unfair, AJ," he says, dismissively.

"Well, that's the law," I state matter-of-factly, and go on to ask him what he wants to do about childcare arrangements.

"Well, fifty-fifty for that; week on/week off, I guess," he replies. "I'm not being one of those dads who only sees their kid every second weekend."

I think for a moment, visualising how it will all work.

"You will need to change your work hours then," I tell him. "So that you can pick her up from after-school club during the weeks you have her. And do school drop-offs."

He stares at me and shakes his head.

"I don't think I'd be allowed fewer hours," he says. "I could drop her at yours on my way to work. Then you could get her from after-school club as usual and I'd pick her up when I finish at five?"

I feel heat rising inside me. "That's not fifty-fifty then!" I argue. "That's me having some custody every day – you'd need to pay more child support for that."

We continue to squabble over all the technicalities until we're interrupted by my phone ringing. It's my sister.

"We can talk about this later," I tell my husband, taking the phone into my room.

"This separation is going to be a fucking nightmare!" I vent to Holly, after she offers her condolences. It obviously hasn't taken long for Mum to spread the word.

"You're doing the right thing," she said after I'd answered. "I know how hard it gets from what it was like with Jeremy," she added, referencing her ex-fiancé.

I tell her about my husband's ideas regarding the split of money and childcare.

"That's total bullshit!" Holly exclaims. "AJ, don't do your own separation agreements – get a lawyer. You need to make sure you get everything you're entitled to."

Before I go to bed that night, I visit my husband in the study.

"What is it?" he asks, his eyes still on the computer screen.

"I'm not discussing anything about the separation again with you," I tell him, my voice calm and slightly cold. "From now on, we will go through lawyers. I'm going to find one tomorrow – you'll need to get your own one as well."

He looks towards me then, seeming a little surprised at my bluntness.

"Okay, fine," he says, shrugging. I turn around and leave without saying anything further, closing the door behind me.

Suddenly you find yourself
ready and waiting
on the other side of the door,
staring out into the unknown.
You ignore the voice telling you
to return to where it's safe –
because isn't safety a compromise,
when you're trapped inside a cage?
So go on, close the door
firmly behind yourself.
Gather all your courage,

and brace for the storm;
but don't give up hope for the sun.
And whenever you feel lost,
be sure to remind yourself,
that although the road's uncertain,
one day you'll find yourself –
somewhere in the unknown.

CHAPTER 29

I Meant It at the Time

On Thursday afternoon, my husband and I both take half days so we can go to our scheduled appointment with Feng before our daughter needs to be picked up.

On the drive to Feng's house where her practice is based, my husband tells me he spoke with a lawyer this morning.

"She said everything does need to be split fifty-fifty, regardless of who contributed what," he says, sounding disappointed.

"I had an appointment with mine yesterday," I say, turning down the car radio. "She said the fifty-fifty thing too. She's going to start drawing up a separation agreement for us and then she'll send it to your lawyer to go over with you."

The lawyers seemed very expensive, but, with likely having saved us countless arguments, worth every penny.

"I talked to my boss too," my husband adds. "He said I might be able to jig around my hours to do school drop-offs and pick-ups from after-school club when it's my week."

I give him a small smile. I'm pleased his lawyer seems to have talked some sense into him. I can't resist prodding him a little, though.

"Well, my lawyer said I could even claim spousal maintenance if I wanted."

I laugh as a look of horror passes over his face. "Don't worry, I'm not going to," I reassure him.

"Men get so screwed over," he says, shaking his head.

"Those laws were created for a reason," I retort. "Just be grateful you won't have to pay for my new shoes and haircuts."

***

Feng greets us with a welcoming smile when we arrive. She looks exactly the same as on her website: a small, pretty Chinese woman, probably in her forties, with long dark hair and glasses framing her sparkling brown eyes.

"Come in!" she says brightly, leading us to a small room just off the main entrance.

We take a seat on the grey sofa, and she sits opposite us in a black leather armchair.

"AJ," she says, "you emailed me saying you've made the decision to separate."

I nod. "Yes," I say. "We have both decided that separating is the best thing to do for us. I guess we thought it might be good to still see you, for some kind of mediation of it all, I guess."

Feng leans back in her chair with her legs crossed and taps her chin with her pen.

"That's a great idea," she says thoughtfully. "We need to acknowledge not only the ending of your existing marital relationship but also look at your path forward in creating your new relationship as co-parents."

Feng asks us to take turns to describe the beginning of our relationship, and why we decided to marry each other.

"It all just felt really easy with AJ back then," my husband says, looking wistful. "I couldn't imagine being with anyone else."

"I felt so certain he was the one and that we would last forever when we got married," I tell Feng sadly when it's my turn. "I meant it at the time."

Feng talks about how people grow and change and evolve, and how, probably at the time, we were exactly right for each other.

"Sometimes, though, we grow in different directions and find ourselves on different paths than the person we were once one with."

She asks us to reflect on the qualities we've been most appreciative of in each other throughout our relationship.

"He's a great dad," I say, glancing at my husband. "He's honest, reliable, and smart and really good around the house. He's a hard worker and kind. We used to have fun back when we went travelling together."

"What about you?" Feng asks my husband. He hesitates for a few moments before responding; I can tell he's finding it awkward to have to express himself like this.

"I've appreciated all the energy AJ has brought to the relationship," he says finally. I give him a look; is that really all he can think to say about me?

It doesn't matter anymore though, AJ, I tell myself before I let it bother me too much.

***

After the session is over, I'm feeling much more positive about the uncertain times ahead. *Maybe we don't have to be a broken family after all*, I think, excited about all the possibilities for us as co-parents.

"That was really nice what Feng said about us creating a new relationship as co-parents, wasn't it?" I ask my husband as he drives us home.

"Yeah, it was," he agrees, his eyes on the road.

In the session, Feng had elaborated on how we could come together as a family sometimes and keep communication lines really open and amicable for the sake of our daughter. It's just reminded me of something; I pull out my phone from my bag and quickly google *conscious uncoupling*.

"Do you remember back in the day when Gwyneth Paltrow and Chris Martin separated, they did that conscious uncoupling thing? We could do that!" I tell my husband a few minutes later, my voice animated.

"Yeah, I think so. What's that supposed to mean again?" he asks.

I summarise my Google findings to him:

"It means to move on amicably and peacefully, with love and understanding and appreciation for each other, even though the relationship didn't work out. It's also about putting a focus on personal growth and healing."

He shrugs. "Well yeah, of course we will try do that," he says, as though the term isn't anything revolutionary to him.

"Yes, it will be really good," I say emphatically. "We could have dinners together, even go on family holidays occasionally…"

I let myself trail off when I notice his eyes glaze over.

"Let's not get carried away," he says drily, pulling into our driveway. "We will see how things go."

As I get out of the car, I catch a glimpse of the bare ring finger on my left hand. It had felt tingly for the first couple of days after I'd stopped wearing my rings. But now it feels like they've never been there.

Not sure when my finger stopped tingling
from the absence of that white-gold ring.
Or when I first looked at our wedding photos,
and realised they no longer captured a thing.
Not sure what I'll do with my dress,
still zipped in a bag and stored away.
Maybe I'll donate it to my daughter's dress-up box,
or I could sell it on Marketplace one day.
Not sure when I broke my promise –
the one I made as I looked you in the eye.
I'm pretty sure I meant it at the time though,
when I told you I'd love you until I die.

CHAPTER 30

Sorry Not Sorry

The next couple of weeks are a blur of lawyer and bank appointments, flat viewings, and telling friends and colleagues our news. Announcing that we've decided to separate has to be one of the hardest parts of the whole process.

"Can't we just put a post on Facebook?" I plead to my husband. I've never been a fan of confrontation.

"No, we cannot," he says firmly. "We need to tell people in person."

But I hate the way they react when I tell them, with a mix of shock and sympathy and curiosity in their eyes. "I'm so sorry! That's just so sad for you all…" seems to be the common response. I can tell they want to know more though; they want all the juicy details, but they don't know what else to say and they're too afraid to ask.

"It's fine!" I reassure them with a cheerful voice. "It was all very amicable."

After applying for several rentals, I'm luckily accepted for the one I had my heart set on – a cute little two-bedroom white-brick unit with an internal garage. It's at the end of a quiet cul-de-sac in a suburb across town.

The settlement figure I've received from my husband gives me plenty to spend on brand-new furniture and things for the house.

"Don't go crazy with it," he warns me, watching me on my laptop as I order a bunch of furniture and appliances to click and collect. "You need to keep some for savings."

"Yes, I know," I say, rolling my eyes.

***

On Saturday, at the end of July, it's finally moving day. Both of our parents have come over to help me move. It's the first time they've all come together since we decided to separate.

"It's all so sad!" my mother-in-law had cried to my mum when she'd arrived, her eyes teary as they'd hugged.

"Oh, I know it is!" Mum had blubbered. "I'm sure they're doing what's best for them though, hopefully it all works out."

My husband and I had stood there in awkward silence as we looked on at the exchange. Our dads were preoccupied discussing the logistics of the move, in typical dad fashion.

My mother-in-law keeps our daughter entertained in the house while the rest of us load my boxes into a trailer and then drive to my new flat and unload it all, as well as pick up the new furniture I'd ordered to collect. The plan is for my daughter to stay here for a few days until I've settled in my new place.

"What else did Vicky say?" I ask my mum, as we arrange the furniture in my new bedroom. Although it's small for a double bedroom, it's light and airy with its cream wallpaper and blush-coloured curtains that frame the large windows.

"She's very upset," my mum replies. "She doesn't think you tried hard enough."

I glance up at her from the box of clothes I'm unpacking.

"But I did try!" I protest, feeling a stab in my chest.

"Yes, I know you did," my mum says softly. "I told her that."

Sorry I'm not the girl he brought home once,
wasn't sure who I was then to be honest.
Quiet and polite, you thought I was a darling,
yes, maybe now I'm not quite so charming.
All I wanted then was for you to like me,
for you to want a daughter-in-law like me.
When it fell apart you said I'd still be family
but we both know that's just a formality:
after all, how could you feel the same
when clearly, it's me who you blame?
I don't expect you to see it from my point of view
when he's your sweet boy who says he loves you
at the end of every phone call
and he's told you I didn't try, but I gave it my all;
just know that I'll never forget your tears at our wedding –
I'm sorry for ruining your happy ending.

***

My husband and his dad head off later once the bulk of the move is done. While my dad sets up my new appliances, Mum and I go to a homewares store where I select a trolley load of kitchenware, bathroom accessories, and other miscellaneous bits and pieces for my flat. It's kind of fun, getting to choose everything myself.

"You must be filling a whole house up," the cashier remarks with a warm smile as she scans through my items.

"She's starting over!" Mum declares in a ridiculous mock-dramatic tone. I laugh awkwardly along with them both, giving my mother a sharp look.

"You didn't need to tell her my life story," I chide her on the way out.

Once my parents have gone that evening, I collapse with exhaustion on my bed. It's adorned with a beautiful new floral duvet I'd bought last week. After a decade of having to compromise with neutral decor colours, it's nice to walk in my room and see roses now.

CHAPTER 31

And Just Like That

*And just like that, the calendar was split,
and I, the constant in your life,
could only see you during the weeks coloured purple.
Those are the days I wear the 'single mum' badge;
the other days I'm just single.
At first, I felt lost in the blankness
of the space you used to occupy,
consuming my time with endless demands;
for playtime and snacks and hugs,
and a bedtime routine that played nightly on repeat.
Soon though I came to appreciate the calm
and relished in coming home to an empty house,
and not having my sleep disturbed
by another one of your bad dreams.
I found myself again,
filling those empty evenings
with the things the me-before-you would've done.*

After a few days in a row of being your mother
and parenting you at the same time
I hate to admit that I look forward to that freedom.
Yet it pains me when your arms won't let go,
and you tell me you miss me before I've gone.
You'll be okay, I tell you,
and myself.
I fight back the tears as I leave you with your dad.
I wonder what I'll do tonight.

CHAPTER 32

Starting Over

Sometimes I cry but my eyes stay dry,
I feel the pain but not the release.
Sometimes I question why even though I know,
the answers won't bring me peace.

Sometimes my grief is deceiving,
because I don't miss what was but what should've been.
Sometimes the sense of freedom is healing,
as I spin towards a future unseen.

Sometimes a voice in my mind says I'm out of time,
it might've been easier to settle for what I had.
Sometimes I have to remind myself that life can't be lived twice,
so that starting over doesn't seem so bad.

CHAPTER 33

A Toast

I let the wine pass my lips,
sweet and indulgent,
yet burns my throat –
a little like freedom.
I drink to raw feelings.
Another sip. I put on music,
turn the bass up loud,
so the drumbeats drown out
the racing thoughts in my mind.
I drink to silence.
I swallow more down
as the sun sets on the day.
A lonely night sets in.
I pull the curtains closed,
and I drink to solitude.
I shiver a little
and curl up in my robe.

*This little flat's draftier
than the house that I owned,
and with the final drop,
I drink to that.
I can breathe here.*

CHAPTER 34

Like Lana Del Rey

I cooked a recipe with coriander;
you weren't here to complain.
I played my favourite music you hate,
like Lana Del Rey.
I forgot to turn off the light
when I left the room.
I don't need you here to remind me –
I'll try break the habit soon.
I climbed into bed later,
and lay down on the right;
the space beside me empty,
just the way I like.

CHAPTER 35

No Destination

After eating my pasta-salad dinner for one, which took substantially more effort to prepare than it did to eat it, I rinse off the dishes and pile them in the sink.

I'll load the dishwasher tomorrow, I think, feeling exhausted. Since I'd dropped my daughter off with her dad that morning (with Saturday being our designated changeover day), it felt like the entire day had consisted of nothing but catching up on chores and clearing up all the clutter accumulated during her week with me. *Is this all my life is now?* I wonder, feeling mildly depressed at the tedium of running a household alone.

I plonk onto the couch, and after switching on the TV for the 'emotional support background noise' I've become dependent on, I check my phone. *That's right*, I think, seeing the unread message in my Messenger inbox – I never got around to reading Ben's message earlier.

Hey, AJ! How's everything going in your new flat? it begins.

It's the first time I've heard from him in a couple of weeks – I guess with everything going on in my marriage, he'd wanted to keep a respectful distance. I read the rest of his message:

I was wondering if you'd like to catch up for dinner sometime once Auckland is out of lockdown? It would be great to see you again. No expectations for anything more x

I reflect on Ben for a moment, and how excited I was about seeing him last time.

Truthfully, he's barely crossed my mind in the last few weeks. While our hotel night was fun, maybe I was projecting on him the kind of connection I was yearning for, to an extent. Plus, he's not even single anyway – now that I'm single, I've realised I'm not really interested in sharing someone with their girlfriend. I tell him it would be nice to catch up and that we will keep in touch. *Maybe there would be no harm in dinner*, I think. But I'm glad he added the 'no expectations' clause.

Switching to Instagram, I reread the message from David I'd received out of the blue last Monday morning. To my surprise, he'd either unblocked me or reactivated his account.

Hey, beautiful AJ! I'm so sorry I just disappeared; things got a bit crazy for a while. I hope you are doing well?

I'd written back, telling him about the separation and how I was on my own now.

Sorry to hear, AJ, he'd said. *I hope you are okay. I still hope to come back to New Zealand one day… Or you are very welcome to come visit me here in Boston xx*

He had asked if I'd been writing poems still.

Not as much as I was, I'd replied. *Maybe I'll try to publish a book of them one day though.*

As I reread our messages from last week, I reflect on my

online affair with David. It seems absurd now; to think how infatuated and absorbed I was with someone I'd never met. *And what was going on with him to fall in love with a married woman across the world?* I wonder.

I decide to check Tinder then. After the separation, I'd tweaked my bio slightly, so it now reads: *Recently separated mum of one. Looking for interesting, open-minded people for fun dates and deep conversations! I love fitness, travel, writing, and nature.*

I've had a few matches, but it seems that a lot of people don't message or don't reply, conversations easily fizzle out, and it's also hard to figure out what exactly I'm looking for.

I swipe fruitlessly through the card stack for a few minutes. *The dating pool here is terrible*, I think, as I realise that I'm up to guys as far away as Auckland already. Auckland is in lockdown right now though, and I'd prefer something local now. Just as I'm about to give up and exit Tinder, Steven pops up. He's forty-four, and apparently only 5km away. He catches my eye with his dark glasses and white shirt. His brown, salt and pepper flecked hair, neat stubble and friendly smile give the impression he's a professional yet down-to-earth Kiwi bloke.

Sunglasses though, they're usually hiding something, I think. But to my surprise, Steven's two other photos reveal kind brown eyes that have a twinkle of mischief.

I can see from his round shoulders he's not in amazing shape, but not overweight either… *Cuddly looking*, I think with a smile. I have a little chuckle to myself when I read his bio:

Seeking fun, casual connections – no monogamy, no shared bank accounts, no expectations.

It's a match! Tinder says immediately after I give Steven a right swipe. I decide I'll be proactive and send the first message.

So, what are *you looking for exactly then? ;)* I tease, referring to his bio.

Steven replies within minutes. It's comforting knowing there are other single people out there probably at home on Tinder on a Saturday night.

Hey, gorgeous! Good question, haha. I'll be honest though – I have four kids from two different relationships, and between two separate parenting schedules I only get one childfree night a fortnight. So essentially looking for someone regular for hopefully hot sex and good adult company every so often. How about you?

I consider Steven's message – something about his self-deprecating honesty pulls me in. I tell him I'm only just out of a marriage and not looking for anything too serious.

You look amazing in your photos, he says, *you must work out a lot? I kinda fell off the wagon but trying to get back into it. What do you do for work?*

I tell Steven about my job and ask him what he does. He tells me he's a recruiter for a temp agency. We continue to chat easily for a while longer, and then Steven asks if I'm free next Thursday night.

I'd love to meet you, he says. *You seem worth spending my one free night with!*

Luckily, it's my week off my daughter, I reply. *Thursday sounds great :)*

***

Thursday doesn't take long to roll around, thankfully. I get an Uber into town to the bar I've arranged to meet Steven at. He's waiting outside the entrance when I arrive.

"Hey, AJ. You're even prettier in person!" he says warmly.

He hugs me, a wide grin on his face.

He's not conventionally handsome, but the mix of his charisma, a deep voice and spicy cologne makes him instantly appealing. In the bar, a waiter takes us to a booth, and we order drinks and a few sharing plates.

"Good choice to come here!" Steven commends me, licking his fingers after a calamari ring.

The date has been easy and fun so far, and even though it's been light-hearted banter and lots of laughs, I can sense that there's a bit of sexual spark there too.

"I've had such a great night," he tells me after we leave the bar. "What are you thinking now, did you want to go somewhere for another drink?"

I check the time on my phone. 10pm already. It feels like the hours have flown by tonight.

"I better not drink more, work tomorrow," I tell him. "But maybe you could come back and hang out at my place?" I'm feeling very bold and flirtatious after a few wines.

"I was hoping you'd take me home," Steven says, giving me a sly smile.

While we wait outside for our Uber, he pulls me in for a kiss. If there were sparks before, they are fireworks now. *This is the best*, I think giddily, enjoying the pressure of his firm hands on my butt cheeks.

***

Thank God I didn't drink even more, I think, staring bleary-eyed at my computer screen. Only 9.45am and I'm struggling to focus, partially from my tiredness and slight seediness from the drinks, and partially from being too distracted by scenes from the incredibly hot sex with Steven on replay in my mind.

My phone buzzes on my desk, interrupting my thoughts. My sluggish brain jolts awake when I see it's from Steven.

Hey, gorgeous, thanks for a great night. You're so sexy. I only just made it into work – I'm fucking shattered, haha.

Steven had slept over after three rounds of sex, and then headed off when we woke up at 7am so I could get ready for work.

For some reason, in Steven's next message, he asks for my email address. *That's random*, I think, but give it to him anyway.

During my morning break, I check my Gmail inbox on my phone and there's a new email from Steven – only it seems to be from his company email address. There's no message, but it has a link to a page titled 'Client Feedback Form'. I laugh to myself when I click on it and realise what he's sent me. *He's so funny sending this*, I think as I type out cheeky answers to the questions:

Job: Hot Date with Steven

Please give a satisfaction score out of 5 for Steven's performance in relation to the following questions (1 = unsatisfied. 5 = highly satisfied). List any additional comments below your response.

1. How satisfied were you with Steven's attendance?
   Score: 5
   Steven arrived punctually at 6.45pm sharp as agreed.
2. How satisfied were you with Steven's presentation?
   Score: 5
   Although clothing was required for only a small portion of the assignment, Steven arrived well dressed in clean business/casual attire. He maintained a clean and tidy appearance at all times even when involved in physically arduous tasks.
3. How satisfied were you that Steven brought the correct tools to the job (if applicable)?
   Score: 5
   While the job brief didn't specify that tools would be required, Steven came well prepared with his own tool, which was appropriate for the nature of the work. He demonstrated an expert level of skill in using this on several occasions.
4. How satisfied were you with Steven's handling of existing company equipment (if applicable)?
   Score: 5
   Although he was a first-timer to my company, Steven handled my equipment with confidence. Though it may have differed slightly from previous equipment Steven had used, he was able to adapt to any variations with ease.
5. Finally, please state how likely you are to hire Steven again (1 = not likely. 5 = highly likely).
   Score: 5
   Steven is welcome back for a hot date anytime!

By the time I click 'submit' at the end of the form, I'm trying to suppress my laughter so hard that tears are running from my eyes. Luckily, no one else is in the tea room with me.

Steven messages me an hour later:

Haha, that's brilliant! I knew you'd nail it… It's gone viral in my office, haha.

Later that afternoon, I get another message from him:

Oh fuck, AJ, that was embarrassing – I had to call the head office in Wellington to get the form removed from the internal server. The IT lady I spoke to was a bit amused!

I snicker as I read it over again. Steven's kind of a mess, but I quite like him, I decide.

Says he's looking for someone to share his life,
no thanks, I'm not ready to be someone's wife.
Says he's lonely on weeknights, wants to stop by,
those are my 'me' nights, I hope he doesn't try.
So many walls and barriers, I'm wasting their time,
all I want is someone who'll come blow my mind.
Then along comes you, straight under my skin,
the perfect drug to remedy this state that I'm in.
Like me, you're a cynic, burnt-out and jaded,
we both know what happens once the passion's faded.
Can't help myself, I jump on board without hesitation,
just want to go on this ride with you
with no destination.

CHAPTER 36

Closure

It's a warm and blue-skied spring weekend, so on Sunday afternoon I ask my daughter if she'd like a visit to the playground.

"Can I get something yummy to eat?" she asks as she puts her sneakers on.

"Maybe we can go to the garden café afterwards," I say, adding, "if you're good and listen to me at the playground." I swore I'd never resort to bribery as a discipline tactic, but it's hard not to fall back on it occasionally – especially now I can't rely on her dad's 'dad voice' to back me up.

When we arrive at the playground, she excitedly runs off to the slides while I watch on from a park bench. I glance around, people-watching for a few moments. It's mostly families consisting of two parents, chatting and laughing as their kids play together happily on the equipment. I swallow and try to brush off the sudden sense of melancholy that hits me – it's a kind of loneliness I hadn't anticipated, being a single mother of a single child at the playground.

I check my phone to distract myself. No messages from Steven since Thursday. But then, I haven't messaged him either, I suppose. He'd been to my house last Saturday night, for Thai takeaways and wine. Then he'd fucked me over my couch, moaning loudly as he clutched my ponytail.

"That felt so amazing," we'd both said afterwards. Then realised we hadn't closed the lounge curtains.

"Hopefully we haven't traumatised my elderly neighbours," I'd said, laughing.

But since then, despite Steven messaging regularly and asking to see me again in a couple of weeks, I'd felt my interest levels wane. Maybe because he became too sexually focussed.

"It would be so hot to watch you with another guy," he'd said. "There's a sex club in Auckland – maybe we can go there for a dirty weekend when it's open again."

"Maybe," I'd said, non-committal. "I think I'm probably a bit vanilla for that stuff though."

My daughter runs over then, pulling me out of my thoughts.

"Can we go to the café now, Mummy? I'm hungry."

***

"Mummy, that man over there looks like Daddy," my daughter says, as we head out of the café after finishing our smoothies and sausage rolls. She's pointing to a table in the corner of the outdoor patio area.

My jaw almost drops when I see the side view of the man she's referring to. He hasn't noticed we're here – he appears to be absorbed in conversation with a dark-haired woman sitting beside him with her back to us. It's a peculiar feeling, to see him in this context. It wasn't so long ago that he was a main character in my life; now here he is, merely one of the extras in the background.

"That man *is* Daddy," I say nervously. "Come on, we should go."

I grab her hand and briskly lead her in the direction of the playground again.

"Mummy! What are you doing? I want to say hi to Daddy," she protests, trying to squirm away.

After I've managed to drag her far away enough that he won't see us, I sit her down on a park bench under a tree.

"Listen, honey, Daddy is with a friend, you won't be able to say hi today," I tell her, knowing it won't possibly make sense to her.

She promptly bursts into tears.

"But I want to talk to *Daddddyyy*!" she cries loudly.

I gather her in my arms and pull her in, smothering her sobs against my T-shirt.

"I… I think he's on date," I say, hesitating. "It wouldn't be nice to interrupt him, but we can visit him later if you want."

"Okay," she agrees, wiping her eyes.

"Let's go on the swings," I suggest, standing up.

Together, we walk back to the playground area and take a swing each. There's something about being on a swing that makes life seem simple and joyful, even in my thirties.

"How high can you go, Mummy?" my daughter asks, looking like she's cheered up a bit.

Lifting my feet off the ground, I push my legs back and forth in the air as hard as I can.

"This high!" I exclaim, tilting my head back to let the wind rush over my face. *It feels like the closest thing to flying*, I think, as I soar toward the sky.

***

"Daddy is taking ages," my daughter complains, a few moments after ringing the doorbell.

"He knows we're coming," I say, pressing it again. "He's probably just on his computer."

An hour after we'd arrived home, I'd texted him, recounting our daughter's sighting of him and his 'lady friend'.

Oh, the poor thing, he'd replied. *I'm home now so you can pop round if you want.*

"Were you on a date, Daddy?" my daughter asks him as soon as he opens the door, finally.

"Yes, I was," he tells her, looking a bit sheepish. "Her name is Michelle."

"Was it a first date?" I ask him.

He nods.

"Well, good thing we didn't hijack it then!" I joke.

"Ha, yeah, that would go down well… Like, 'Nice to meet you; here's my ex-wife and my daughter by the way,'" he says, laughing.

"I'm going to go play," our daughter informs us, skipping off to her toybox.

I suppress my urge to ask my ex more questions about Michelle… *How old is she? What does she do? Does she have kids?*

It's not really my place to know everything now, I remind myself.

"I'm finding dating a bit harder than I expected now I'm an actual single person," I admit.

"Why is that?" he asks.

I think for a second before I respond.

"It just seems like guys on the apps in my age bracket are either looking for a casual hook-up, or our parenting schedules usually clash. Or, if they don't have kids already, then they are looking for someone to start a family with."

I turn my eyes towards my daughter and watch as she carefully dresses her dolls. No longer helpless and completely dependent on me, but an almost independent, fully autonomous person.

"I'm not sure I could go through all that again," I say, my voice tinged with a sad resignation.

My ex shakes his head. "Having a second child was never on the cards for you, AJ."

"Maybe not, I don't know," I say, shrugging.

We talk for a while longer and I find myself venting to him about some issues at my work, like old times. Then I tell my daughter we need to make a move so I can start dinner.

"I'll miss you, Daddy!" she says, hugging him goodbye.

I watch in the rear-view mirror as he goes inside and closes the door to my old house.

"Alright, let's go home then," I say to my daughter, buckled up in her booster seat. She seems happy again now, thankfully.

"It's all going to be okay," I promise her as we drive back to her other life, and the new version of me.

Closure

I felt it as I chatted to him in his kitchen;
he was like an old friend yet a new acquaintance.
Part of him had broken with our relationship;
and the rebuilt parts of him seemed inaccessible.
I liked this new version of him though;
that I could only view from a distance.

I felt it as I exploded into a monologue
about my stressful week at work, our daughter…
and every other frustration, while he nodded in understanding.
He was always a good listener –
but suddenly it felt strange; for him to be 'that person'
for me still.

I felt it as I realised that one day someone else will be there,
listening to me patiently while I vent.
Someone who understands me more than he ever did.
And maybe there'll be someone in his kitchen
who knows the new him more than I ever will.

I felt it then – closure.
An acceptance that we've arrived on the last page
of our final chapter together.
Ready for our new stories.

About the Author

The Undoing of My Marriage is the debut book of AJ Moore (a pseudonym), a New Zealand writer and poet.

AJ began writing it a couple of years after her marriage ended, while still adjusting to life as a divorced single mother. While the story is true to her experiences, names, locations, and identifying details have been changed.

Although the book was written retrospectively, the poems featured in each chapter were first composed in real time, serving as emotional timestamps from the period that marked the 'undoing' of AJ's marriage.

AJ's poetry collection continues at her website ajmoorewriting.com, where readers can also find an intimate note from her and see the woman behind the words.

To connect with AJ or for media enquiries, send a message via the contact page on her website or email her at ajmoore@ajmoorewriting.com.

If you're curious about what came next for AJ...

Written shortly after her debut, AJ's companion novella *Not a Fairytale Ending: The Rewriting of My Story* takes readers behind the scenes as she writes – and rewrites – *The Undoing of My Marriage*, while also navigating the third year of a physically intense but emotionally volatile 'casual' relationship she can't seem to let go of.

With the same candour and vulnerability as her debut – but from a deeper perspective – *Not a Fairytale Ending* explores the addictive pull of inconsistent intimacy, the erosion of self within imbalanced connections, and what 'finding yourself' after divorce really means.

Not a Fairytale Ending is available as a free ebook via the Not a Fairytale Ending page at ajmoorewriting.com.

To download your copy, enter the password **fairytale2025**.